# A Christmas Cruise Murder

## Dawn Brookes

# A Christmas Cruise Murder

A Rachel Prince Mystery

Dawn Brookes

Oakwood Publishing

Paperback Edition 2019
Kindle Edition 2019
Paperback ISBN: 9781913065041
Copyright © DAWN BROOKES 2019
Cover Design: Janet Dado

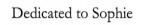

Dedicated to Sophie

# Contents

Chapter 1 ................................................................. 1

Chapter 2 ................................................................ 10

Chapter 3 ................................................................ 20

Chapter 4 ................................................................ 32

Chapter 5 ................................................................ 41

Chapter 6 ................................................................ 51

Chapter 7 ................................................................ 60

Chapter 8 ................................................................ 70

Chapter 9 ................................................................ 81

Chapter 10 .............................................................. 87

Chapter 11 ............................................................. 100

Chapter 12 ............................................................. 111

Chapter 13 ............................................................. 121

Chapter 14 ............................................................. 133

Chapter 15 ............................................................. 145

Chapter 16 ............................................................. 156

Chapter 17 ............................................................. 167

Chapter 18 ............................................................. 176

Chapter 19 ............................................................. 185

Chapter 20 ............................................................. 194

Chapter 21 ....................................................... 206

Chapter 22 ....................................................... 216

Chapter 23 ....................................................... 226

Chapter 24 ....................................................... 233

Chapter 25 ....................................................... 243

Chapter 26 ....................................................... 252

Chapter 27 ....................................................... 262

Chapter 28 ....................................................... 270

# Chapter 1

The *Coral Queen* London tour bus was parked outside the Natural History Museum, the last stop before returning to the ship. Rachel showed her ticket to the driver, who loaded her suitcases into the luggage hold. Delighted she was to be taken directly to the cruise liner, Rachel found the one remaining seat next to an older man who reluctantly removed a bag to allow her just enough room to sit.

"Thank you." Her smile was met with a hard stare followed by a brusque reply.

"You're welcome," he answered in a thick Spanish accent while sniffing through overly wide nostrils that reminded her of those belonging to a friend's bulldog. The man turned away from her. There was welcome in neither his voice nor his actions.

The bus set off, slowly at first due to London traffic, but it picked up pace as it got further away from the centre. It was carrying a mixture of passengers and crew, taking back-to-back passengers and off-duty crew members on a tour of London before picking up additional passengers and heading straight to the port in Southampton.

Rachel could see the rain had become heavier than it had been when she'd stood waiting for the arrival of the bus, a typical English winter's day with temperatures hovering at around five degrees centigrade outside. There was a palpable buzz in the air and she could hear the two people occupying the seats in front of her discussing their Harrods purchases. Rachel sat back and relaxed. Her night-duty shift had only finished at seven o'clock this morning. Since then, she had raced home, grabbed a few hours' sleep and telephoned her fiancé, Carlos, who had gone to Italy to work on a last-minute case over Christmas.

As a private detective, Carlos took the work when it was available, but he wouldn't have taken a case over Christmas if he had not been cajoled by his cousin to do some undercover work for her. She'd explained that items were being stolen with increasing frequency from her hotel and she suspected there was an insider feeding information to the thief or thieves. Her main concern was that the hotel would lose its good reputation and be tarnished by the robberies.

Rachel had been bitterly disappointed, but had hidden it well when Carlos told her he wanted to go. They had both been looking forward to spending Christmas together, as Rachel, being in the police force, worked most Christmases.

"Why don't you use your compensation money and join Sarah on a cruise?" Carlos had suggested.

Rachel's best friend Sarah worked as a nurse on board the cruise ship Rachel was now heading towards, on which she had become embroiled in a number of murder investigations on previous sailings. Some of them had resulted in generous compensation from the cruise line.

"But her parents are joining her this Christmas; I'd feel like I was intruding."

"I'm sure they would be happy to see you, and Sarah would definitely be pleased."

"I suppose it beats Christmas at the vicarage. Dad is always so busy during the holiday season and Mum ends up feeding the waifs and strays with nowhere to go. I don't mind that usually, but I really wanted a rest. I've been working flat out since I became a DC."

"Not to mention your sergeant's exams."

Rachel had been thrilled to pass first time and was applying for DS jobs, so it wouldn't be long before work became even busier.

"You're right, a cruise would be nice and the Christmas one is only for twelve days. I spoke to Sarah about it the other day; she was excited, but nervous about her parents taking a winter cruise."

Carlos had looked relieved when she'd capitulated. She knew he felt guilty for leaving her and ruining their holiday plans. The sparkle in his eyes as he grinned triumphantly had brought the familiar butterflies to her stomach.

Rachel had made a last-minute booking just a few days ago. She'd dropped Carlos off at Heathrow before going on nightshift the previous evening. Now she texted him to let him know she was on the coach, then texted her parents. Afterwards, she looked across the man next to her to glance out of the window and couldn't help noticing him scowling and muttering to himself.

"Are you alright?"

"Yes, why shouldn't I be?" His tone was no friendlier than earlier.

"No reason, sorry. It's none of my business. My name's Rachel, by the way. Are you on holiday or working?"

"Working," he answered glumly. "I am maître d in restaurant on board ship."

Rachel knew Colin Bell, the maître d from the main restaurant, but hadn't met this man before, so she wondered if he was new.

"How exciting, that's a responsible job, isn't it? Making sure food is delivered on time and diners are happy."

He turned and looked at her for the first time. A short man with jet black hair and nostrils that were still flaring, he appeared to be in his late fifties with a deeply lined face and marked frown lines indicating he was probably not the happiest man in the world. His eyes were too small for his face and almost got lost in his large head.

Through tight lips, he answered, "It is responsible job, I have to keep difficult waiters in order."

"I see," she replied, not quite sure how to continue with this conversation, whether to bother or where it was going. It seemed the man was now on a roll, so she didn't need to ponder for long.

"They hate me, but I don't care about them." He huffed as he blew out the final part of the sentence.

"Hate is a strong word, I'm sure they understand you are just doing your job if you have to be firm at times." Rachel thought he probably ruled with a rod of iron judging by his general demeanour, but then she knew nothing of managing waiters from all over the world so reminded herself not to judge.

"Strong word it may be, but they do hate me. Anyway, they have to lump it, as you British say. I'm not going anywhere – they will have to take me off in a box." His voice rose as he spat out the last words and laughed insincerely.

Rachel chuckled politely. "I'm sure they wouldn't want you to leave. I expect you're very good at what you do. Which restaurant do you oversee?"

"Are you familiar with *Coral Queen*?" he asked.

"Yes, I've cruised a few times before."

"I used to be in specialty dining, now in Club Restaurant."

"I haven't heard of that one."

"That's because it is new addition – a meeting room

has been converted to make room for restaurant. The cruise line wanted to offer somewhere different for higher paying passengers, but for this cruise it is being used for anyone who wishes to book." He again spat the last part of the sentence out.

Rachel raised an eyebrow but resisted rolling her eyes. The man next to her was clearly proud of his position in the new restaurant, but didn't approve of its use for this sailing. At least she had managed to distract him from frowning momentarily.

"I am Stefan Sosa. Perhaps you will be dining in my restaurant, Miss?"

Rachel hoped not. "Perhaps."

"That's if the waiters don't kill me first." He attempted a laugh that came out as more of a groan and caused him to go into a coughing fit. Once he had recovered himself, he turned away again and looked out of his window. "Rain, always raining in England. No wonder you British are so unhappy."

*As opposed to your ecstasy,* she thought, but said, "We're used to it."

"Being unhappy?"

Rachel laughed. "The weather."

She was saved from any further conversation as they entered the outskirts of Southampton and the passenger across the aisle asked her the time. Rachel happily engaged in conversation with her and her husband for the remaining fifteen minutes before they pulled up beside the enormous cruise ship that always took her breath away.

Stefan pushed in front of her while she helped an elderly woman on with her coat. Rachel sighed and hoped that would be her last encounter with maître d Stefan Sosa.

As she reached back to collect her bag, she noticed a small brown wallet sticking out from the back of the seat where Sosa had been sitting. She picked it up and looked around to see if she could chase after him. There was no way – the aisle was now filled with passengers keen to alight from the coach. Looking through the window, she saw him gesticulating and shouting at an older passenger on the portside before he stormed off towards the crew-only entrance. She sighed and stuffed the wallet into her handbag.

*I'll hand it in on the way in.*

Stefan made his way to his room and ordered room service, despite knowing that he shouldn't do so as embarkation day was the busiest day for catering staff and waiters.

"I don't care how busy you are, I need food now. I wasn't going to pay London prices and I've not eaten all day. Get on with it – that's what you're paid for."

He slammed the phone down and grinned at the idea

of creating extra work for the lazy kitchen staff.

Shortly after his food arrived, Stefan sat down and poured himself a glass of whisky, even though he would be working soon. This was something he always did; rules were not for him.

"What do I care?" he muttered out loud. "I'm the boss."

He thought of how different things had been since he had suffered a minor stroke sixteen months ago when on leave after a row with his family. He hadn't declared the stroke on his return to ship and the crew doctor – Romano or whatever his name was – hadn't picked up on it. However, it had left him with a permanent limp. No-one had asked him where the limp had come from and he had become more and more bitter with each passing day; nobody cared about him and he certainly didn't care about them.

He hated working in 'service'; he should have been a senior manager by now, but had been passed over again and again for younger men, and recently by a stupid woman. That rankled more than anything. In Cuba, women did as they were told, but not here. Here they got senior jobs and told him what to do.

*Stefan Sosa will never take orders from women; they have to be kept in their place.*

It had been a frustrating day, but he had got his point across to that his ex-wife of his. No-one could hide from him forever; he would make them all pay. Stefan glared at the dinner in front of him, thrown together and presented poorly. He would make the staff suffer for this later, too.

"At least the bread looks fresh," he muttered. He added more whisky to the glass and lifted it into the air, waving it around in a salute. "To hell with the world," he shouted as he downed the contents and bit into the bread.

As soon as he swallowed the first bite, he felt pain in his stomach and tightening in his throat as the swelling in his airways appeared from nowhere. His gut burned and he slammed the bread and his glass down on the table. Panicking, he reached inside his pocket for his epi-pen.

It wasn't there.

He stumbled to the dressing table and opened the drawer. The pens were not there. Clutching his throat as the wheezing became louder, he tried to suck in air, scowling as he fell to the floor. One of them had finally made good on their threats.

Stefan fought to take one last breath, but it never came.

# Chapter 2

Sarah Bradshaw was filled with excitement this morning, knowing her parents would be joining the *Coral Queen* for the first time. Not only that, but her best friend Rachel had booked the same cruise at the last minute after discovering her fiancé would be working while Rachel herself had been given the Christmas season off. It was the first time her friend had had time off over the festive season since she'd joined the police force; Sarah was sorry Carlos wasn't coming too, but other than that she couldn't be happier.

The ship had just returned from a three-week cruise taking in the Adriatic Sea, Greece and parts of the Mediterranean. Crew had been exceptionally busy with a fully booked voyage and the medical team had worked flat out. A number of passengers from the same extended family had caused the team problems with boisterous and demanding behaviour; they seemed to think they could monopolise the health centre throughout the three weeks. Knowing that the troublesome family had disembarked this morning added an extra spring to Sarah's step.

Sarah arrived in the medical centre where she passed

through the waiting room into the storage room. She was singing out loud while stocking up medicines from there into the treatment rooms when the familiar teasing voice of her friend and colleague, Bernard, took her by surprise.

"Who let the cat out?"

"What are you doing here? I thought I was getting some peace and you were going into Southampton this morning."

"I was, but have you seen the weather? It's pouring down. I don't like your English winters, it is never like this in the Philippines."

"From what I hear, the rain can be much worse in your country. Monsoons, I think you call them!" Sarah was always happy to banter with Bernard who was like a mischievous teenager at times, despite being older than she was at thirty-four.

"Ah yes, but then our rain is followed by beautiful sunshine, something your country knows little about." He stroked his chin as he continued with a small sigh, "Although I concede our floods can be horrendous at times. Anyway, back to why I'm here. I didn't feel like going out today; I was tired this morning and slept in. Brigitte kept me up late, moaning as usual about everything in the world. She was feeling so bad she drank one of my stingers without even realising it. She will have a bad head today, that's for sure."

Bernard's stinger was his top-secret cocktail recipe and not a drink for the fainthearted. Every so often, he would challenge crew members to taste it and guess what was in it – a pointless exercise as he wouldn't tell them even if they were right.

"Brigitte wouldn't normally touch your toxic cocktail – she must have been in a bad way."

"She was in a right state. After complaining about the horrible Munro family, she went off on one and started moaning about men…" he rolled his eyes "…again, and how awful we all are."

Sarah laughed. Bernard was frequently on the receiving end of their French colleague's tongue lashings when it came to the frailties of men.

"Now what has the masculine race done?"

"It seems she has had another row with Novak. Not her fault, of course – it never is – and now she's off men forever, she told me. We're all the same: selfish – I won't use the word she used, but you get the picture. They will be together again by tonight, I'm sure. She's such a firebrand, that one, I don't know how he tolerates her."

"Who tolerates who?" Gwen, the senior nurse, joined them in the treatment room.

"Brigitte. It seems she and Novak have had a fight and Bernard was dealt the punishment for it."

"Ah," Gwen recognised immediately there was no malice in Bernard's comments as he and Brigitte had a topsy-turvy but positive friendship. Gwen strived for a happy team and they were pleased to oblige. "Did all the medicines arrive?"

"Yes, I was just checking them in and stocking up when Bernard joined me."

"Why aren't you in Southampton, Bernard?"

"Hangover," answered Sarah, shooting him a challenging glance. "He tried to blame the weather, but I know better."

"It's hard being the only man in this team, and therefore a punch bag." He pouted his lips, folding his arms across his chest for effect.

"You've got Graham and Alex, what's the matter with you?" Gwen retorted.

"I know, but they're doctors. I'm just a lowly nurse."

"Now that is a first," laughed Gwen. "And long may you remember that moment of humility, Nurse Guinto. Right, I'll leave you to it. I'm going to meet with Graham before the next lot of passengers arrive." Gwen slapped Bernard on the back as she left. "Think yourself lucky we've got rid of the Munros."

Bernard smirked and mock wiped his brow. "They're history, I've already moved on." He had found the Munros even more difficult than the rest of the team as one of the older women had become infatuated with him and seemed tuned in to whenever he was on duty. In the end, he'd asked for a chaperone, which Fern Munro had not taken to kindly, but she'd eventually got the message. Although he was happy to flirt, he was renowned for being faithful to his wife and loved his three children.

Bernard turned to Sarah after Gwen left. "Do you

want me to help in the passenger lounge later? I don't think Brigitte will be up to much. We should let her lie in – not to mention she'll owe me one if I take her place. By the way, why were you so happy when I came in? Has Jason proposed?"

Sarah stared at him in disbelief. "Why do you think?"

Bernard slapped his head. "Of course, your parents are coming to the Canaries with us, and Rachel's joining the ship. That means we'll have a Christmas cruise murder to look forward to." He ran out of the treatment room, rubbing his hands together before Sarah had the chance to rebuke him.

"One of these days, Bernard," she shouted after him.

Two hours later, Sarah and Bernard were checking health questionnaires in the passenger lounge off ship while she kept her eyes peeled for any sign of her parents or Rachel. Rachel was coming directly from London so would arrive separately by coach. Her parents were driving down from Hertfordshire and leaving the car at the port for the twelve-day cruise.

As she had passed through the main atrium of the ship to exit, Sarah had been delighted to see the gigantic Christmas tree dominating the space. There was a happy hum in the air as excited staff rallied around, putting up decorations and generally making the passenger areas look as good as they could for the time of year. Thankfully the weather forecast was for relatively calm seas over the next few days, assuring them of a decent passage across the Bay of Biscay, which could be a challenging crossing when seas were rough. Many a passenger had stories to tell of hair-raising cruises, and Sarah was worried her mum might get seasick on her first cruise and it would put her off, but decent weather was reassuring on this front.

"Sarah!"

Sarah looked through the sea of passengers heading towards the security desk and recognised her mother's straight dark-brown hair, perfectly aligned an inch above her shoulders. Her father was behind her with the hand luggage.

"Go," said Bernard, "I'll manage."

Sarah made her way through the bustling crowds and hugged her mother, then her father.

"Oh, Sarah, you look beautiful in that uniform. The photos really don't do it justice." Her mother stood back to examine her. Sarah blushed, pleased at the effusive greeting. There was a time when Mary Bradshaw hadn't approved of her daughter working on board a cruise ship, constantly reminding Sarah that she would find it difficult to settle down. Sarah hadn't wanted to settle down and had fought hard for independence, but rather than argue, she'd reassured her mother that when the time was right, there wouldn't be any problem. She hadn't believed her own words, so she was certain her mother hadn't been taken in by them, especially when Mary reminded Sarah – and anyone who would listen – that cruise ship nursing was just a phase she needed to get out of her system. And then, after a few short and meaningless relationships, she'd met Jason on board the ship, and soon afterwards everything changed and everyone was happy.

Sarah turned to her father, who smiled warmly, pride written all over his face. "Well, Officer Bradshaw, what do we do next?"

"Follow the queue, Dad. I've got the evening off so I will come to your stateroom to collect you before the official switching on of the Christmas lights in the main atrium. We're dining in the Club Restaurant tonight. It's a bit quieter there – a new addition to our dining choices."

"Will Jason be joining us?"

"Yes, for tonight, but he has to work the nightshift afterwards." Jason and Sarah had been seeing each other for nine months, and they were growing closer with each passing day.

"That all sounds wonderful. Now don't let us keep you from your work." Forever the pragmatist, her mother clearly realised Sarah had left her post. "I take it that's your friend, Bernard, over there – the one with the cheeky grin? I recognise him from the photos you showed us."

"That's him. I'll introduce you to the team tomorrow. Graham – that's Dr Bentley – has invited you to join us in the officers' dining room tomorrow evening. Sorry, I hope that's alright? I can put him off, if you'd prefer."

"We wouldn't dream of it. We look forward to meeting all your friends and colleagues. It will be good to be able to put faces to the names and remember the characters when we're back home, and it will cheer your mother up to know that you've not been kidnapped by pirates."

Sarah's father appeared as excited as her mother. It was going to be bliss having them on board. They all laughed at the joke, recognising that her mother's biggest fear when Sarah had joined Queen Cruises was that she would be kidnapped off the coast of Somalia and be held for ransom or sold into slavery. Around the time she'd accepted the job as a cruise ship nurse, there had been a number of high-profile kidnapping and ransom cases where yachts had been boarded by modern-day pirates, causing Mrs Bradshaw countless sleepless nights. It was only after Rachel had been on board and assured Sarah's mother that ship security was exceptional and the security crew were well trained and prepared to repel any attempt at piracy that she had stopped worrying about it. Even so, Sarah's father vetted the newspapers before showing them to his wife, particularly when Sarah was on a world cruise.

Sarah watched her parents pass through security and waved before rejoining Bernard and concentrating once more on the passenger questionnaires. During a brief gap in passengers boarding, Bernard spoke.

"Your parents seem happy to be aboard."

"They are. I so want Mum to enjoy the cruise so that she can accept my job choice. She was proud when I became a hospital nurse, but seems to see cruise nursing as a lesser career choice somehow."

"I thought she was happier now you're with Jason?"

"That has helped, certainly. Particularly as he's English – no offence, Bernard, she's not racist, but I'm an only child and she would hate it if I moved to another country to marry. She's rarely been abroad and doesn't really like travelling. I think that might have been an added fear when I took the job – that she would have grandchildren over the other side of the world."

"Perfectly understandable. I would feel the same if it was my daughter, even though I only see the family every nine months in between contracts."

"I don't know what she'd say if Jason decided to rejoin the army, though. I don't think he'd be quite the hit he is now."

"That's not likely, is it?"

"Jason still carries a lot of baggage from his time in Afghanistan, so I guess not." Sarah wished she could help her boyfriend recover from the memories that plagued him, but he was not yet an open book on that topic. On top of that, she was well aware that he still had trust issues over his fiancée breaking up with him after his second tour abroad, leaving him heartbroken and almost costing him the ultimate price as he lost the will to live for a while.

Bernard, aware of the tensions in the relationship and how Sarah walked a fine line with Jason, gently squeezed her arm.

"You'll make it. Both of you will."

# Chapter 3

Rachel sat on a comfy chair drinking strong coffee as the ship departed Southampton. The view through the balcony windows was obscured by raindrops creating patterns on the expansive glass and she watched them bouncing off the balcony table outside. The rain was still coming down heavily, grey skies and mist obscuring any further view as they left port in the twilight, although she could make out lights from smaller boats sailing on the Solent.

With the dark nights of winter, there would be less opportunity for the evening walks on the upper decks that she so loved when cruising. It would put a different perspective on things, of that she was certain. She hoped there would be some clear skies as they moved south so that stargazing could be an alternative evening entertainment.

*Somehow, Rachel Prince, you're going to have to buck yourself up and enjoy the holiday*, she chided herself.

After closing the thick, heavy curtains and turning her attention to unpacking, she paused to tap FaceTime on her iPhone and call Carlos who answered immediately.

Seeing his face cheered her up immensely.

"Hello, Rachel, how was your journey?"

"Very straightforward as it happens. I think I'll take the bus more often – unless Marjorie's with me, that is. Then it's chauffeur driven every time." Lady Marjorie Snellthorpe was an octogenarian whom Rachel and Carlos had become close to and who loved cruising as much as Rachel now did. They had met during Rachel's first cruise when Marjorie had been pursued by a hitman.

"I bet you've already made new friends." He grinned and his bright brown eyes flashed with affection.

"Not yet. I sat next to a grumpy man on the bus who works on board – a maître d. He did nothing but moan all the way down. Thankfully it was a short journey."

"Ha, if you couldn't make him happy, there's no hope for the man. Have you seen Sarah yet and how does the ship look?"

"No to the first question. I'm waiting for her to call, and the ship is wonderful as always. It looks even more spectacular for this cruise, as you would expect. There's a huge Christmas tree in the main atrium; I can't wait for the switching on of the lights later. There will be a ceremony hosted by the deputy captain once the safety drill's over."

"That sounds exciting. I wish I was with you."

Rachel sighed. "Me too. How's the investigation going?"

"I've not really got started yet. I met with my cousin,

Chita, this morning and she filled me in on what's been happening. The thefts occur at various times of day or night, but always out of sight of CCTV, which is why she believes there's insider involvement."

"Sounds like it could be, but it could just be a thief that's done their homework. Does she have any ideas or suspects?"

"Nothing concrete. I have a list of staff that started work here in the last six months and I will delve into their records tonight. Chita has given me the paper personnel files and I can do background checks from my room. We've decided to pretend we don't know each other so as not to arouse suspicion. I don't think it will take long to wrap this one up."

"I like your optimism. What's the hotel like?"

"It's good quality, a nice place. I would say it's a bit like a posh golfing hotel you would get in England. She's done well for herself, but reputation is everything in these parts."

"Well, good luck with it, you'll get it solved in no time, I'm sure. I'll contact you in three days when we hit Lisbon. I'm not paying for Maritime roaming or Wi-Fi access, the prices are extortionate."

"Be careful in Lisbon, remember what happened last time."

"Oh, you're right. I had forgotten about that. Thankfully Marjorie's not here, it was worse for her." Rachel shuddered as an unpleasant memory from her first cruise invaded her mind.

"Sorry, I shouldn't have brought it up. Forget it. Ciao for now, I love you."

"Bye, darling, I love you too. And Carlos?"

"Yes?"

"Take care."

He nodded, blew her a kiss and she tapped out of FaceTime just as the telephone in her room rang.

Rachel spotted Sarah's parents, standing among the crowds in the huge atrium, waiting for the Christmas lights to be formally switched on. Sarah was unmistakable in her lily-white officer's uniform. Rachel sidled up behind them and tapped her friend on the shoulder.

After delighted hugs and greetings, they were silenced as the cruise director's voice burst through the loudspeakers.

"Good evening, ladies and gentlemen, welcome aboard the *Coral Queen* for this very special Christmas sailing. This is the first time we've sailed from the UK in the winter months and we very much look forward to providing you with fun and activities throughout your stay with us. Now, I'm sure you all want to explore the ship, so without further ado, I have great pleasure in introducing our master and commander, Captain Jenson."

Loud applause and cheers filled the room, which spanned two decks. Every available space was taken, even on the stairways.

"I thought it was going to be the deputy?" Rachel whispered to Sarah.

"It was supposed to be. Captain Jenson obviously trusts him to assist the pilot now we're past the smaller boats. The pilot does most of the work anyway when we're leaving port."

"Thank you, Carla." The captain's voice boomed as he took the microphone. "That was Carla Tewitt, our cruise director. She and her team will ensure that the entertainment on board is of the highest quality. Now, ladies and gentlemen…"

The captain went on to give a welcoming speech, introducing his senior officers including Dr Graham Bentley, the senior medical officer who Rachel knew from previous cruises, and chief of security, Jack Waverley, who she also knew, but hoped she would not have too many dealings with during this sailing.

"We will be sailing to Lisbon, followed by Madeira, La Palma, Gran Canaria and Lanzarote, with Christmas Eve in Lanzarote and Christmas Day on board the magnificent *Coral Queen*, so if you weren't expecting to be in any of those places, you're on the wrong ship."

Laughter filled the room.

"The weather forecast is for brightening skies as we reach the Bay of Biscay and mild winds with a moderate swell as we cross through. Nothing to worry about. I will keep you updated with weather announcements each day, but the long-range forecast for our stops is promising with highs of twenty-one degrees centigrade during the day. You can expect six hours of sunshine during most of our Canary Island stops.

"Now it is the moment you've all been waiting for: time to switch on the Christmas lights." Captain Jenson pressed the button on a remote control and the atrium lit up to the sound of bells and rapturous applause.

Rachel stared up at the wonderful tree, which was taking centre stage, while listening to a string quartet playing in the background. Sarah's face lit up as the twinkling from the larger tree lights danced in her recently highlighted light-brown hair. Passengers clapped again loudly before dispersing in the direction of the main restaurant or the theatre, depending on whether they were booked on first or second dinner sittings.

"What happened to Gordon?" Rachel asked Sarah when she could be heard above the noise of milling passengers.

"Who's Gordon?" asked Gilbert Bradshaw.

"He was cruise director for a while, Rachel met him before." Sarah cast a warning glance towards Rachel so that she wouldn't reveal the circumstances involved murder. "He decided to return to Wales and see his nephew through university, they have become close. We think Gordon has also met someone new, although his divorce isn't through yet."

"I'm pleased for him, he deserves a bit of luck," said Rachel.

"Carla was the assistant cruise director and deserving of the promotion. Better late than never, if you ask me."

"I remember seeing her around previously. Anyway, I'm hungry. Where are we eating?"

"I've booked us a table in the new Club Restaurant for dinner. Shall we go?" Sarah said excitedly. Rachel inwardly groaned at the thought of meeting up with the miserable Stefan Sosa again, but didn't want to put a dampener on Sarah's mood so she nodded enthusiastically.

Gilbert Bradshaw took his wife's hand and the trio followed obediently behind Sarah. Jason was waiting nervously outside the restaurant and held out his hand towards Sarah's father.

"Mr Bradshaw, good to meet you again." Sarah had taken Jason home to meet her parents during her last break and had reported to Rachel that the visit had been a resounding success.

"Good to see you too, Jason. You can dispense with the Mr – call me Gilbert."

"And please call me Mary," said Sarah's mother as Jason leaned down to kiss her on the cheek.

"Hello, Rachel." Jason pulled her into a hug while Sarah chatted to her parents, and whispered, "Glad you're here to help steady my nerves."

"You've nothing to be nervous about. I'm reliably informed you are quite the hit with the Bradshaws."

Jason beamed and stood straighter, showing off the muscular frame beneath his uniform. Her friend had not only picked one of the nicest men she'd met, but also a handsome one, Rachel thought happily.

The group was led through a well-lit room, where diners were already seated, to a table for five in the centre of another long and narrow room. There were tables for two next to windows, currently screened by curtains to hide the black night outside. The ship rolled a little as they walked, taking Mary by surprise and she lost balance momentarily. Jason was quick to support her and he and the waiter ensured she was seated safely.

"I'm afraid a winter cruise might not have been the best choice for your maiden voyage, Mum, sorry."

"Don't you worry about me. I'll get my sea legs soon enough, I'm sure." The flicker of concern in Mary's eyes as she glanced towards her husband told a different story. "At least I don't get travel sick as a rule."

"No you don't, Mary," Gilbert said reassuringly as he too took his seat. Rachel looked around for the maître d she'd met earlier, but there was no sign of him.

*I'm sure he said he was working tonight.*

"Are you expecting someone, Rachel?" asked Sarah.

"Not really. I met the maître d from this restaurant on the bus coming down, but I haven't seen him this evening. I thought they always took names when people entered the restaurant."

"You're right, he's not here. No wonder the waiters are so chirpy."

The waiters did seem to be happy, introducing themselves as they handed out the menus to passengers, and there was a warm atmosphere around the room.

"Waiters on board the *Coral* are always happy and friendly," Rachel said.

"There can sometimes be a tense atmosphere in Stefan Sosa's restaurants – he can be a bit of a taskmaster. I'm sure he's around somewhere. Do you want me to ask?"

"Oh no, don't worry. He didn't seem to be the happiest person I've ever met, so perhaps he's unwell."

"Is someone unwell, madam?" A tall waiter had appeared, carrying a jug of iced water, and heard the last part of the conversation.

"No-one's unwell, Pash. Rachel met Stefan on the bus coming down from London so we were wondering where he was," explained Jason.

"Oh really? That's interesting, we thought he might have missed the ship." Was there a hint of disappointment in his tone? "In that case, I don't know, madam. He hasn't turned up for shift. We called the maître d from main dining and he told us he'd let us know where Stefan was later, but to get on with it for now. No word since."

"I expect everyone's busy because of turnaround day, I'm sure you'll hear soon enough," said Sarah.

"Yes, first night is always busy – as you know, Nurse."

"Pash?" asked Rachel after the waiter had left.

"Short for Pashmarli – Pashmarli Bakshi. Everyone calls him Pash, even says that on his badge," Sarah explained.

An attractive wine waitress arrived shortly afterwards, followed by another good-looking waiter offering a selection of breads. Mary Bradshaw was inquisitive about the workings behind the scenes on board ship and quizzed Sarah and Jason throughout the meal, while Gilbert listened on, taking it all in.

"I'll give you a tour of the ship while you're on board so you can see what goes on. Be prepared to be amazed, Mum. Jason's even arranged for you to visit the bridge."

"Now that would be interesting, Jason, thank you," said Gilbert. Jason blushed and acknowledged the thanks with a nod.

The waiters were attentive and helpful. Rachel watched them go about their work efficiently, but felt they were a bit like swans on the water: calm on the surface while frantically moving underneath. There were eight waiters that she could see working across the three separate spaces, and she spent a few minutes trying to guess where they all came from.

Pash was Indian – she'd seen that on his badge the next time he'd come to the table following their initial conversation. The wine waitress, Danielle, was from Portugal and a couple of waiters looked Serbian or

Croatian. The tall, handsome waiter called Sacha who served most of their food was from Russia, according to his badge. There was another Indian or Pakistani waiter and the other two looked central European.

"Rachel?"

"Yes?"

"You're miles away. Mum just asked where Carlos was this Christmas."

"Sorry, I was trying to work out where the waiters are all from. It's a game I play when I cruise."

"Yes, then she moves on to the passengers," laughed Sarah. "Her mind never stops whirring."

Rachel smirked at her friend. "Says the person who remembers dates like a calculator! Anyway, in answer to your question, Mary, Carlos is in Italy working on a case."

"Over Christmas?" Gilbert exclaimed.

"That's what I said when he told me, but he's doing a favour for a cousin, and Christmas is all about family after all." She sighed heavily.

"Well I agree with you there. What about your parents?"

"They'll be busy with Christmas services and feeding the five thousand."

"Yes, we did feel slightly guilty about leaving them in the lurch, but they understood. We haven't seen them for a few weeks." Gilbert took a sip of his red wine.

Jason looked uncomfortable when the conversation turned to family. Rachel knew that family life for him hadn't been easy, but didn't know the details. Now he was obviously waiting for the attention to move towards him and she suspected he was dreading being asked about his own family. Jason was outgoing with Sarah, but she sensed he was shy of her parents, even though they were doing their best to put him at ease.

As Mary Bradshaw turned to him with mouth open, ready to ask a question, Sarah cut her off at the pass.

"Mum, we need to get moving if we're going to get seats for the show."

As Jason squeezed her arm in gratitude, his radio beeped.

"Sorry, I have to go. Something's come up." He kissed Sarah on the forehead and left the restaurant.

# Chapter 4

Jason arrived outside the crew member's room on deck six just as Dr Graham Bentley was leaving. The doctor shook his head as the two men passed each other, standing to one side as a wheeled stretcher was brought out by Bernard and the medical team steward, Raggie. Whoever was on the stretcher was covered by a blanket and Bernard's slit throat action indicated what Jason had already surmised: whoever was beneath the covering was dead.

After the medical team had departed, Jason entered the room to find his boss going through the scene.

"Fatality, I'm afraid, Goodridge."

"Is there anything suspicious, sir?"

"Not that I can see. At first glance, it appears the man had a severe allergic reaction to something he ate. The strange thing is he was allergic to nuts, which catering staff are well aware of, and he hadn't used any of his epipens according to the good doctor."

"Where was he found?"

"On the floor just there." Jason followed his boss's gaze towards the desk attached to the wall. "The drawer where the epi-pens are kept was open so he may have been trying to reach for one, but the reaction came on too quickly and was too severe for him to make it in time. As you can see, the pens haven't been used."

Jason noted how tidy the room was apart from an overturned chair next to the desk, presumably knocked over when the man had reached for the pens. It reminded him of when he was in the army and he wondered whether the dead man could be ex military.

"Who found him?"

"One of the catering staff, Claudia Kitova. She was sent to find him by the head maître d, Colin Bell, when he didn't turn up for work in the Club Restaurant."

"Was it Stefan Sosa?"

"Yes, did you know him?"

"I've never met him, but we were just talking about him over dinner. It seems Rachel Prince met him on the bus on the way down."

Jason knew he had said the wrong thing as soon as he saw the redness travelling from Waverley's neck up to his face, the groan coming from his boss's mouth confirming it.

"Oh no. Why does she have to be in contact with every single death that occurs on this ship? I do hope for all our sakes there is nothing untoward about this unfortunate incident. It seems pretty straightforward."

Waverley stared as if in a trance at the half-eaten slice of French bread on a plate. Jason noticed nothing else had been eaten. It suddenly dawned on him that Waverley's new wife was senior baker and managed the part of the bakery where bread was prepared for special diets. Waverley started to sweat as though the thought was occurring to him at the same time. Taking a handkerchief from his pocket, he mopped his brow and turned to Jason.

"Deliberate or accident, if it came from our galley, heads are bound to roll."

"Yes sir, I guess so. Although he had been off ship so he could have picked something up there. Shall I bag the bread, sir?"

With a long exhaled sigh, Waverley nodded. Jason could see his boss's neck pulsating. He donned gloves and bagged the half-eaten baguette, then picked up an empty glass and sniffed.

"Whisky. This could have clouded his judgement. I thought he was supposed to be working tonight?"

"He was. Drinking on duty is a sackable offence, not that we can do anything about it now. It could affect his insurance cover, though, if he'd breached the terms and conditions of employment. We'll see if alcohol is found in his system. Perhaps he did eat something on land he wouldn't normally." Waverley sounded hopeful and Jason fully understood why.

"I'll bag the glass, sir. Do we need to seal the room for SOCO?"

"Yes, I suppose we do for now. Did Rachel Prince say

anything about his mood on the bus? I'll have to interview her, of course, and that's likely to trigger her snooping gene. Blast! Why did it have to be her?"

"She has been helpful to us in the past, sir."

Waverley sighed again. "I know she has, but this one could be personal, Goodridge. You know what I mean. I'd just rather have as few people involved as possible in case it turns out to be a catering error, that's all."

"I understand," Jason said. "What did Claudia Kitova have to say about the whole thing?"

"I don't know." Waverley scowled. "Graham tells me she's too distressed to be interviewed, so he's sedated the woman and I won't be able to speak to her until tomorrow – if I'm allowed to speak to her at all."

"What do you mean?"

"Don't you see, man? If there's any suspicion of Brenda having prepared that bread and if it contained nut traces, I will have to exclude myself from the investigation. Personal involvement and all that, you know how it is."

"Have you asked Brenda about it?"

"Not yet, I've been too busy here. I think it best if we go to the galley together once we've finished preliminaries. She'll be devastated."

"What about a post-mortem?"

"The pilot's still with us and has requested a sea ambulance to collect the body and transport it back to England for PM."

Jason had wondered why he'd felt the ship slow down towards the end of dinner; now he understood. His boss looked seriously worried and he couldn't reassure Waverley as there was no evidence of anything else Stefan Sosa might have devoured other than the bread and the whisky. No wrappers in the bin, no sign of food in the drawers, or anywhere else in the poky little minimalistic cabin.

At least it was a one-person habitation, so no roommate to worry about re-homing while they investigated. As a maître d, Stefan had his own room at the end of a corridor on deck six, well above the waterline. Jason as an officer had a balcony room further along the same corridor, and Sarah had a similar room further down. For once, Jason was hoping that this was murder because the thought of Brenda losing her job and what Waverley would do then filled him with dread.

"The man wasn't popular, from what Sarah was saying over dinner, and the waiters in the Club Restaurant appeared happy he wasn't around. I think it would be worth interviewing some of them as well as Rachel."

"That's a very good idea. I'll go and speak to Rachel Prince first, then we will go together to see Brenda. I think you should start with his work colleagues in the morning."

"They'll be serving breakfasts, but I could pull them out one at a time, I guess."

"Right, you go to the medical centre now while I track

Rachel Prince down. Hand over those things before the ambulance arrives and see if Graham can add anything to this story. And check if he still thinks anaphylaxis is the cause of death."

"Yes, sir."

Jason headed towards the medical centre with the evidence bags that would accompany the body to the coroner. When he walked through the door into the centre that housed a waiting room, reception desk, surgery rooms and an infirmary, he heard Dr Bentley's voice coming from Gwen Sumner's office. Gwen and the chief medical officer were becoming close according to Sarah, but were not romantically involved as far as she knew.

Gwen, the senior nurse, was an Australian who didn't pull her punches when required and was well respected by the medical team. Firm but fair, Jason understood. Bernard was the joker in the team, Brigitte the more serious one and Alessandro Romano, the junior doctor, was hard working and great with kids and crew.

Jason knocked and entered as Gwen called for him to come in. Bernard was sitting on the sofa while Gwen and Dr Bentley were in the chairs surrounding a table holding freshly poured cups of coffee.

"Hello, Jason, would you like a coffee?" Gwen greeted him in a friendly manner. "I expect you're here about Stefan Sosa."

"Yes please, and yes, I am. Sorry to bother you, but

I've brought these things to accompany the body." Jason placed the bagged items on Gwen's desk and sat down next to Bernard. "And the chief wanted to know if there was anything to add."

Graham Bentley looked tired. "Sad business, so needless if only he'd used his epi-pen. I'm certain it was anaphylaxis. The swelling is consistent with a severe allergic reaction and I can't see any other cause of death from my preliminary examination. I just don't understand how it happened; his allergy was well known to him, and to the catering staff. The tray of food in his room had the right sticker applied; it's an absolute tragedy. A complete waste of a life."

"Did he have any other allergies, sir? Wasps, bees, anything like that?"

"Not as far as we are aware, and such insects aren't around at this time of year, but I get your point. The only thing listed in his medical record is severe nut allergy. He had epinephrine pens in his drawer and would have been told to carry one with him at all times."

Jason took notes. "Was there any sign he'd used one of his pens?"

Dr Bentley looked at Bernard. "You were there first, Bernard. I didn't see any used pen, did you?"

"No sir, none on or near his person. It looked as if he had got to the drawer but not managed to take a pen out. We gave him adrenaline from our emergency bag, but it was too late."

"Is it unusual that he didn't get to use his own pen?" Jason asked. "The drawer was very close to the dinner tray."

"As a matter of fact, yes, it is unusual. He should have had time to get to the drawer and inject himself, but that is the only odd part about it all."

"He had been drinking whisky, I believe, sir."

"Ah, well that could have made a difference – depending on how much he'd drunk, of course. Alcohol does tend to slow one's responses. That might explain it. I did note from a recent consultation with Alex that he had warned the man about the demon drink; Sosa had raised triglycerides following a routine cholesterol check. Alex had requested he return for liver function tests." Graham Bentley drained his coffee and Gwen refilled his cup.

"I concur with that," said Bernard. "Sosa was a known drinker; I warned him about it many times myself when I saw him for routine checks. He also had a limp, so that might have slowed him down."

"I don't suppose alcohol could have caused his death?" probed Jason.

"Sorry, no. A contributing factor perhaps if it prevented his ability to administer life-saving injections, but not causation. You see—"

Jason could sense Graham was about to launch into a medical lecture, which ordinarily he would have found interesting, but in this instance he wanted to get to the bottom of the case and help his boss.

"Could he have eaten anything containing nuts off ship and reacted later?"

"Not if he'd eaten nuts. His allergy was too severe, but there's always a possibility he'd developed a second allergy to something else and that could have caused a delayed immune response. We'll know more after the post-mortem, but for now we have to assume that he somehow imbibed nuts or nut residue from what he was eating in his cabin."

"That would be terrible," said Gwen. "Brenda always checks off food given to passengers and crew with allergies. She's very strict about it, and we provide regular training to all the catering staff on prevention of cross-contamination, as you know. Even when she doesn't bake the bread herself, she marks every ingredient down on charts and staff undergo rigorous training on maintaining an audit trail, so it will soon come to light if there was an error. Jack must be worried sick."

Jason grimaced. "It is obviously a cause for concern."

"Perhaps it will turn out to be that he ate something different," said Bernard. "Are you sure there's no foul play? Rachel Prince is on board, after all."

"Trust you to joke about it, Bernard," Gwen scolded.

Jason drained his coffee cup in one mouthful and stood up.

"That's what we intend to find out."

# Chapter 5

After taking a stroll around the outside decks after dinner, Rachel walked along the corridor back towards her stateroom. She felt tired, the nightshift catching up with her, and looked forward to getting a good night's sleep.

It came as a surprise to her to see the chief of security, Jack Waverley, hovering outside her door. His face was expressionless, although she could tell from the redness in his neck that something was amiss.

"Chief Waverley, what a pleasure to see you again. How are you?"

"I'm sorry to disturb you, Miss Prince. May I have a word?"

Rachel knew from the nervous cough preceding the sentence and his formal use of Miss Prince that this was business rather than pleasure. She frowned, puzzled.

"Of course, do come in." She opened her door and walked towards the sitting area at the far end of the room, feeling Waverley hot on her tail. "Can I get you a drink?"

"No, thank you, I'm on duty."

"What about tea or coffee?"

"No thanks."

"Do please sit down. What can I help you with?"

Rachel was dumbfounded. What could the reason for his presence be? He appeared nervous.

Suddenly she felt a surge of panic. "Is everything alright at home? Are my parents okay – please don't tell me something has happened to them or Carlos!" She felt her chest tighten and palpitations surge through her body.

"No, no. I'm so sorry, I didn't mean to distress you. Please don't be alarmed, it's nothing personal like that. I do apologise, I should have asked how you were and reassured you that it was nothing to worry you. I'm a little distracted." He did appear agitated, so she understood. "I just wanted to ask you a few questions about a man that Goodridge tells me you met earlier today on the bus before you joined the ship."

"Thank heavens!" Rachel felt herself relaxing, but decided to pour herself a martini from the mini-bar before sitting opposite the chief. "The only person I met was a maître d called Stefan Sosa. I take it that's who you mean?"

Waverley coughed. "Precisely. I'm afraid Mr Sosa was, erm, unfortunately found dead in his room earlier this evening and I was wondering if you could shed any light on his mental state when you met him. I assumed from what Goodridge told me that you'd had a conversation with the man."

"You could call it that. We introduced ourselves,

passed the time of day and spoke briefly, but to be honest, I wouldn't describe it as a conversation. He came across as a rather unhappy man, though, if that helps. How did he die?"

"We're not certain. It appears he had an anaphylactic reaction to something he ate, as far as we can tell at present. Did you notice him eating anything while you were travelling?"

"Nothing that I saw. He slept part of the way and gazed out of the window. I would have noticed if he'd eaten anything major, but I couldn't tell you for certain. He may well have sucked a sweet or popped a toffee in his mouth, and I wouldn't necessarily have seen that. I texted Carlos while we travelled so may have been distracted. He did appear to be muttering to himself quite a bit, which I found odd."

She noticed a flicker of hope appear in Waverley's eyes and wondered what he was hiding. Of course it would be easier if the man had eaten something on the bus that later caused a reaction, but still, Waverley was not his usual self.

"Did he have known allergies?"

The cough told her that Waverley was indeed concerned about something else. "Yes, he was allergic to nuts and nut residue, peanuts in particular, but he was on a special allergy diet." He coughed again. "It looks as though it might have been the bread."

Rachel nodded sympathetically, immediately

understanding why he was so concerned. Waverley's new wife worked in the ship's bakery, but that didn't mean she was the one who had made the mistake.

Waverley ran his hand through his thinning hair. His hairline seemed to recede with each cruise she took; she hoped the two things weren't related.

He rose to leave. "I don't suppose he mentioned anyone threatening him at all?"

"I don't see why he would tell me anything like that, chief. Surely you don't suspect foul play?"

He looked down, forlorn. "Not really, but it can't be ruled out just yet. There is something else odd. He had anti-allergy pens within reaching distance and yet he didn't use them."

"Perhaps the reaction came on too suddenly, or perhaps he was so unhappy he decided to end it all in the only way he knew how."

"Well if he did, he changed his mind. He was found on the floor with the drawer containing the pens open."

"People do change their minds, chief. It wouldn't be the first time."

"You could be right." Waverley's shoulders slumped and he took a deep breath.

"Actually, thinking back, he did speak quite bitterly about his colleagues a few times. Said they hated him, and he may have half-joked about them needing to kill him if they wanted to get rid of him, which suggests he wasn't contemplating suicide, but who knows? I don't remember exactly what he said; he appeared a bit paranoid and I was only half listening. I couldn't take to him, but I wish I'd paid more attention now."

Waverley's head jerked upright, but then his shoulders slumped again. He walked towards the door.

"I have taken up enough of your time; I'll leave you to it. Thank you for your assistance."

Rachel stared at the back of the door after the security chief left. CSO Waverley had become a friend of sorts over the past few years and she had never seen him looking so down. He was usually confident and bullish, even when she disagreed with him, but the man who had just left her room looked defeated. What was that all about? It could just be the fear that his wife or another member of the crew had made a terrible mistake, but this reaction belied a deeper fear – one that she would like to help him with. But how?

Jack Waverley's head was down as he walked towards his office. Jason had been waiting outside for half an hour and couldn't help wondering why his boss wanted him to accompany him to interview Brenda. If it had been Sarah involved, Jason would want to speak to her alone before any investigation was launched. He'd want to reassure her that she had his full support, whatever happened. This behaviour was slightly out of character for the chief who, although he dotted the i's and crossed the t's, would also do his utmost to protect his own, which was why Jason liked him so much – they were both loyal.

Waverley ambled along slowly, looking like he had the weight of the world on his back. He appeared not to see Jason and headed straight through to his office.

"Er, hum."

Waverley jumped and turned around. Was that a tear? Jason's heart beat a little faster. What the heck was going on?

"Ah, there you are, Goodridge. Come in."

Jason flicked the light switch as his boss walked heavily towards his desk in the dark. "Sir, are you okay?"

Waverley didn't lift his head, but flopped down in his chair, ignoring the question. "What did you find out?"

"Dr Bentley is convinced it was an anaphylactic reaction and that it occurred suddenly. He says Sosa would have died within minutes, but he won't know for certain until after the post-mortem. The body and the evidence were due to leave the ship a short while ago. I felt the ship stop so I expect it's all on the way to Southampton now. The doctor did also say he was a known drinker and concurred the whisky might have affected his judgement and ability to react, but—"

"But what?"

"I worked with a lot of heavy drinkers in the army, sir, and there are many on this ship. Those who drink like that can behave perfectly normally with reasonable

46

reaction times. Having said that, we don't know how much he'd had to drink. He could have been on a binge in London for all we know."

"Quite. Has the man's son been informed?"

Jason had received a call from Gwen Sumner while he was waiting for the chief, informing him that Sosa had a son listed as next of kin. How come his boss knew that? Perhaps he was testing him.

"Dr Bentley has phoned the son, yes."

"Was he alright?"

"The son or Doctor Bentley, sir?"

"The son," Waverley snapped.

"I don't know, sir. I understand from what Gwen told me that he's studying at Exeter University and, from Dr Bentley's conversation with him, she surmised that they weren't close, but that's all I know."

"Yes, he has a promising career ahead of him, I believe, studying physics. Wants to work with nuclear energy. Why anyone would want to do that is beyond me."

Jason's mouth dropped open. "Is there something going on here I should know about, sir?"

"Not yet, Goodridge. It might not be relevant anyway. Now let's go and interview the bakery staff, shall we?"

"Including your wife, sir?"

"Yes, Goodridge," Waverley sighed heavily, "Including my wife."

Jason followed his boss out of the chief of security's

office, feeling like he was missing something that formed part of a bigger picture, but it seemed Waverley was deliberately keeping him in the dark, so he wasn't sure whether he wanted to know. Surely his boss wouldn't be covering anything up?

He kept in step with the chief while mulling things over in his mind. Of course Waverley would be worried. If his wife had made a fatal error, it could cost Brenda her job, but why did Waverley know so much about the dead man's son? What else did he know that Jason didn't? Jason tried to reassure himself that Waverley was testing his thoroughness in case he had to drop out of the investigation rather than the alternative: that his boss might be part of some sort of conspiracy.

They arrived at the galley and passed chefs, galley staff and waiters going about their nightly duties. Dinner was well over, although the buffet staff would still be working upstairs. Here, though, the bakery was in full flow. It was almost midnight and the nightshift bakery staff were starting on fresh bread, rolls, pastries and other delicacies ready for the breakfasts.

A flustered woman who Jason hadn't met before was in the allergy section of the bakery as they arrived.

"Stop right there," she commanded.

Waverley drew to a halt and stared down at the round woman dressed in whites, hands on hips, sternly blocking his path.

"I need to speak to the bakery staff that were on duty

around early dinnertime."

"Well you won't find them here. Don't you know what time it is?" she answered brusquely, her Scottish accent becoming more pronounced as she raised her voice.

"Perhaps you could provide me with their names, then, and I will need the meal preparation list that was sent up to Mr Sosa at around five-thirty."

"Oh, him. Yes, of course, I heard he'd died. I shouldn't think it's any great loss, although I don't like to speak ill of the dead. What's that got to do with his meal? I thought it was a heart attack."

Waverley tensed. "That's for me to know. Please just give me what I need."

"Alright, no need to bark. Wait there." The woman's chest heaved up and down, affording Jason a brief glance at a badge revealing her as the bakery supervisor before she bustled away from them.

Jason couldn't resist chuckling to himself. He had never heard anyone speak to his boss like this woman had just done, and the redness rising from the chief's neck to his forehead confirmed that Waverley was not used to it either. If Waverley hadn't been so worried, Jason was certain he would have put the woman in her place, but as it was, this was turning out to be no ordinary situation.

The evening supervisor returned, breathless, with a piece of paper in her hand. "Here is the staff list, the details of what was ordered by that horrible man…"

*Clearly not speaking ill of the dead,* Jason thought.

"...the food that was plated, and who delivered it to the room. I can tell you now, though, chief, our procedures are rigorous. None of the food prepared here would contain anything he was allergic to, if that's what you're thinking, and you of all people should know that."

At this point, she puffed out her chin, defiantly challenging Waverley to contradict her.

"Thank you for the information," Waverley replied timidly, concentrating on the list he had been given.

Almost as soon as the two men left the kitchen, both of their radios sounded.

"Captain requests your attendance on the bridge."

The message was the same for each of them. Jason looked at his boss, who managed a grim smile before marching towards the lift in the staff area leading up to the bridge. Jason followed in silence. He would find out soon enough what this was all about.

# Chapter 6

Rachel's instincts told her the death of Stefan Sosa was not down to chance, but whether it was murder or suicide she wasn't entirely certain. It seemed an odd way to commit suicide. She had come across diabetics who overdosed on insulin and those who stopped treating themselves, but she hadn't heard of anyone deliberately giving themselves anaphylaxis.

She was also worried about Waverley and the implications for him if his wife had made a mistake. Would Brenda get the sack, and if so, what would that do to Waverley's career? Waverley was in his fifties, but didn't appear to be a man considering retirement.

These thoughts prevented her from going to bed after the chief had left. Strictly speaking, it was none of her business and the sensible thing would be to leave well alone, but since when had she done the sensible thing when there was a puzzling death to be solved? She resolved to sleep on the matter and see what the morning brought.

After finishing a second martini, she was just about to get ready for bed when she remembered the wallet she had found on the seat of the bus.

"Drat! I should have handed this in." She took it out of her handbag, opened it up and checked the contents.

An hour later, Rachel was still mulling over what she had found.

*I should show it to Waverley, but it's too late now.*

She stared at the door card in her hand and sighed. There was no way she would sleep until she'd checked Stefan Sosa's room for herself, but she couldn't go alone. She remembered Jason was on duty, but didn't know where security hung out at night. Reluctant to page him, she picked up the phone and dialled.

A sleepy voice answered. "Hello?"

"Sarah, sorry to wake you. Can I come down?"

"Rachel, it's two o'clock in the morning! Are you ill?"

"No, I need to speak to Jason, but don't know how to get hold of him. Can you ask him to meet us in your room?"

Her friend sounded fully alert now. "Whatever this is about, I don't like the sound of it. Tell me why?"

Rachel explained about Waverley's visit and the death of the maître d. Sarah hadn't heard about it as she had accompanied her parents to the evening show, being off duty, and had headed straight to her room afterwards.

Then Rachel told her about what she had found on the bus. "So, you see, I need to speak to him. I don't want to wake Waverley; I want to take a look in the man's room, preferably with Jason. The wallet contains Sosa's room card. I could go alone, but I'd rather not."

"No, you certainly must not do that. I'll call Jason and have him meet us. Give me half an hour to shower and dress."

Rachel returned the phone to its cradle and noticed the message light flashing.

*That's odd, Sarah didn't tell me she'd called earlier.*

She lifted the receiver again and pressed the button, recognising the voice straight away.

"Rachel, I'm sorry to bother you, I realise you are on holiday, but I have friends aboard the *Coral Queen* who may be in danger. I'll call again in the morning to explain further. I realise you won't have a mobile signal over the next few days, but I can contact you via the purser's office. God bless. Goodnight."

Rachel listened to the message again a couple of times before heading off to Sarah's room.

Half an hour later, Rachel, Sarah and Jason were sitting around a coffee table, drinking strong coffee. Jason had arrived in Sarah's room just before Rachel; he looked tired, but he also looked stressed. Rachel wondered if he already suspected something.

"Before I tell you what I've found, I must ask that you don't tell the chief just yet, because it implicates his wife and I can't quite get my head around it. My first reaction was to tell him, but now I don't think that's wise."

Rachel noticed Jason stiffen and the frown on his face became even more pronounced than it had been before.

"I didn't think this night could get any worse," he groaned. "Ordinarily I would refuse your request, but the chief is off the case so I'm not obliged to inform him of anything that relates to it."

Both Sarah and Rachel stared at Jason in disbelief. "What do you mean, off the case?" asked Rachel.

"Just that. Captain Jenson summoned us both to the bridge around 12.20am just after we'd been to the galley. The captain was none too happy as he'd found out that the dead man was Brenda Waverley's ex brother-in-law and there had been animosity brewing between them."

Jason put his head in his hands for a moment and sighed before taking a gulp of coffee and looking up again.

"Stefan Sosa had been married to Brenda's sister, but they divorced. It seems he was violent towards both her and their son. Brenda persuaded her sister to leave him long before she met the boss, and the sister, Christine Sosa – now Christine Jones, and their son Mikey did a bunk with Brenda late one night while Sosa was at work. They stayed hidden in a relative's country cottage while acrimonious divorce proceedings went through.

"That was ten years ago. Mikey is now Michael Jones, having taken his mother's maiden name. However, he was listed as Sosa's next of kin – a recent change, I'm told

– so the deceased obviously knew about the name change and where Michael could be found."

"I see," said Rachel thoughtfully. "So I take it, if this all happened ten years ago, that the divorce wasn't the end of it?"

"No, Sosa plagued his ex-wife through a mutual friend, who agreed to deliver his letters but not divulge Christine's address. At first the letters were pleading, spelling out Sosa's love for her and their son, requesting access to the boy which had been denied by the courts – that sort of thing. When the letters became more threatening, the mutual friend refused to deliver any more and there was no contact for seven years, until very recently."

"Is that why Sosa went to London yesterday?" asked Rachel.

"I think so. I haven't had a chance to interview Brenda yet, but I suspect he contacted Christine again before his demise."

"Did Waverley know about any of this?"

"He only heard about the history when he became aware that Brenda never spoke to Sosa, despite them both being involved in the catering side of things. He didn't know about the recent contact, but I think he suspected something, either immediately or shortly after the man was found dead and it appeared the kitchen staff might be implicated in his downfall."

"No wonder he looked so worried." Rachel was

saddened by the whole situation.

"So, Rachel, what have you discovered and why does it implicate Brenda?"

Rachel explained how she had picked up the card wallet after Sosa exited the bus and had meant to hand it in, but forgot all about it on boarding. Then later, when Rachel met up with Jason, Sarah and her parents, it had slipped her mind again.

"I couldn't sleep after Waverley left and I had a nagging feeling about the death of this man. I was about to go to bed when I remembered the wallet. As well as a room card, it had this inside."

Rachel handed Jason a folded piece of paper and he read the contents grimly, tightening his grip around the note.

*Look here, Sosa,*

*It's time you moved on and stopped being the brute you are.*
*Be reasonable and stop contacting my sister and stay away from my nephew.*

*I'm warning you for the last time. Leave her alone or you'll be sorry.*

The letter was unsigned, but it was clear who it was from.

"This doesn't prove anything," Jason said.

"I agree, on its own it doesn't, but with the death of the man it was addressed to and in the light of what you've just told me, it's pretty damning evidence."

Jason's head dropped. "I don't believe it. There has to

be some other explanation."

"What are we going to do about it?" asked Sarah. "We can't show it to Waverley and I don't think the captain should see it, at least not for now."

"You're asking me to withhold evidence. You know I can't do that." Jason's eyes darted from one woman to the other.

"Not permanently," said Rachel. "Just until we can find out who killed the man, because I don't believe for one minute it's the person who wrote that note. From the sounds of it, he was a nasty piece of work, and he did admit to me that everyone he worked with hated him. I thought nothing of it at the time, but what if someone really did dislike him enough to kill him?"

"Okay, I'll hold on for now, but don't give it to me. I think you should hang on to it for now, and we'll discuss this again tomorrow." Jason handed the note back to Rachel, who took it, folded it and returned it to the card holder.

Jason kissed Sarah on the head. "I need to get back or Ravanos will be wondering where I am, and I want to check the records of anyone who worked with Sosa. I'll be interviewing the waiters in the morning."

"Remember to get some sleep," Sarah called after him.

After he had left, Rachel turned to Sarah.

"I still want to look at the room."

"Why didn't you ask Jason?"

"I was going to, but to be honest, I think he's got

enough to process, being suddenly left in charge of the investigation. If we find anything else incriminating, we need to tread carefully. I don't want to compromise Jason's loyalty or put him in an impossible situation."

"Well I'm coming with you."

"Before we go, there's something else."

"Oh no, Rachel, no more evidence, please."

"No, it's totally unrelated. After I called you, I noticed there was a message on my stateroom phone. It was Marjorie; she says she has friends on board and thinks they might be in danger."

Sarah shook her head. "I don't believe it! Neither of you can stay out of trouble for one minute, can you? Who are these people?"

"I don't know, she didn't say. She said she'd call again in the morning via the purser's desk. If Marjorie's concerned, she must have good reason to be."

"But why didn't she tell you before you left?"

"That's the bit I'm not sure about. I spoke to her two days ago to wish her a happy Christmas and to give her my and Carlos's whereabouts over the next few weeks. She's been invited to her son's for Christmas Day, and then she's going down to Cornwall to see a cousin for a week. There was no mention of her friends being on the same cruise, let alone being in danger."

"Perhaps she's only just found out."

"You're right, that must be it. I remember she told me and Carlos about a month ago that she had recommended him to some friends, but as far as I'm aware, they didn't contact him. I wonder if it's related to that."

"Trouble just follows you around, doesn't it?" Sarah laughed.

Rachel nodded and managed a smile. "I guess it comes with the territory."

"It doesn't mean you have to be involved in every crime committed within a twenty-mile radius, though. Why didn't you mention it to Jason?"

"Sarah, you saw the look on his face. He's gutted about the Waverley thing. I'll discuss it with one of the security team once I know more in the morning – if there's anything to discuss, that is. Perhaps it might give Waverley something else to think about."

"Anyway, there's nothing you can do about it for now, so let's get this room search over with. Tie your hair up and keep your head down. At least the room is on my corridor. I'll check the coast is clear, then we need to walk quickly and confidently."

"Sarah Bradshaw, you're becoming quite the detective."

Sarah giggled. "At least if we're caught, we'll only be reported to Jason."

# Chapter 7

Rachel followed Sarah along the silent corridor housing officers' and senior staff's rooms, trying not to appear conspicuous. Sarah paused, and then stopped outside Sosa's room where Rachel used the key card she had found in his wallet to open the door. They had opted not to use Sarah's universal swipe key in case it logged her entry; Rachel was keen not to get her friend in trouble, especially if Captain Jenson was already tetchy about the potential involvement of the CSO's wife.

The room was pitch-black before Sarah turned on the lights. Inside, the stateroom was small and airless, cramped all the more by a double bed dominating the space. A small table and two armchairs where Stefan must have eaten his last meal were visible in the corner.

A desk with two drawers was fixed to the wall opposite the bed and behind the table. One drawer was open, revealing the unused epinephrine injection pens still lying there, and an overturned chair suggested that was where Sosa had met his end.

"This room's a trifle claustrophobic," said Rachel.

"Not as bad as those below the waterline, though."

Sarah shrugged her shoulders. "At least he had his own shower and toilet; the waiters will be in shared rooms, remember?"

Rachel did remember having been in one of the crew members' rooms below the waterline – or below stairs, as she liked to call it – on a previous cruise, and Sarah was absolutely right. That room had been a poky excuse for accommodation with bunk beds and very little furniture, and barely enough room to turn. There, the two occupants shared a shower and toilet with those from the room next door.

"You're right, this is luxurious by comparison." She shuddered at the thought of being in yet another dead crewman's cabin. At least this one didn't reek of cigarette smoke; just whisky. "Anyway, let's get started. You check the bedside table while I look over here." She walked towards the desk with the opened drawer.

"Hang on a minute, Detective Prince, you'd better wear these." Sarah handed her a pair of surgical gloves.

"Thanks, good thing we have the same size hands. I was going to use a plastic bag, but these are much better. I think I've told you before, nurses would make great criminals."

Rachel opened the drawer next to the one already open, after checking there was nothing but the epinephrine pens in the first. The next drawer contained a hair dryer, phone charger, some loose change in a neat pile and some blank postcards. She sighed.

"Nothing here. What about you?"

"Only this," Sarah handed her a battered old address book. There were addresses from all over the world, including many from Cuba.

"Was he Cuban originally? His accent sounded Spanish, so that would fit."

"I'm not sure. Definitely South American, so possibly Cuban. I only remember seeing him once; he always insisted on seeing a male nurse when he attended check-ups, so we gave him Bernard. We try to accommodate." Sarah rolled her eyes.

"And now we know he was a misogynist wife-beater, that fits his profile," said Rachel.

"He must have had dual nationality, though, if he lived in England."

"I'm sure he did. A lot of these addresses based in Cuba could be family members; they have the same surname, although I'm not sure how common the name Sosa is in Cuba. It could equate to Smith or Jones in the UK, for all I know."

She leafed through the book and stopped at a page. "This is the only recent entry I can find. No name, but a London phone number and a mobile number crossed out. I'm betting the number belongs to his ex-wife, Brenda's sister."

Rachel took a photo of the entry with her mobile phone. Walking towards the built-in wardrobe, she announced, "I'll check his clothes."

Sarah yawned loudly and sat on one of the chairs. "You'll have to be quick. I'm done in and I've got to do a surgery in a few hours."

Rachel smiled sympathetically at her friend as she opened the wardrobe door. The wardrobe was organised with military precision: jackets, then shirts, then trousers.

"Well, well, our Mr Sosa was very precise." She began rifling through Stefan's pockets. "It always feels wrong, going through a dead person's things, but I seem to be doing more and more of it nowadays."

"Especially when you come on board the *Coral*," Sarah teased.

There was nothing of any significance to be found in any of the clothes Rachel examined, just a few mints and the odd till receipt neatly folded and placed in an upper pocket of a jacket.

"Nothing. Hang on a minute, what about the safe? Any idea what his date of birth was?"

"None, and I'm not ringing Jason to find out."

"What about reception?"

"No way."

"Come on, Sarah, think!"

"I could go down to the medical centre and pull up his records. Rachel, can't this wait until morning? I'm shattered."

"Okay, but let me just try something first." She tapped in the numbers 1, 2, 3, 4 and smiled gleefully as the safe opened. "Got it." She pulled out a pile of papers and photos. "I'll take these back to my room and go through them there so you can get to bed."

Sarah smiled gratefully as Rachel walked over to where she was sitting and plonked herself on the other chair, taking in the room in more detail. "Have you noticed anything odd?"

"The only odd thing I've noticed is the two of us in a dead man's room in the middle of the night. Thank goodness it's not Halloween."

Rachel chuckled. "Besides that?"

"No, I can't say I have. I take it you're going to tell me sometime before breakfast?" Sarah yawned again.

"The room's immaculately tidy, almost OCD tidy. Even the contents of the drawers are in neat piles – the money, the postcards. The wardrobe is colour coded, everything in order except for one bit."

"The epi-pens." The realisation dawned on Sarah. "They're not aligned."

"You're right, Watson, which suggests?"

"That someone else put them there, Sherlock."

"Either that or Waverley fiddled with them when he found the body. We'll have to hold on for the answer to that question."

"Sosa could have done it himself trying to grasp one of them. Do you think it was murder, then? I was rather hoping it was a neat little suicide."

"I'm not certain, but it's an odd way to kill oneself, isn't it? I think a man as regimentally minded as this would have at least moved the pens and stacked them neatly out of reach before doing himself in. Also, why would he call his wife and threaten her if he was planning on suicide?"

"Assuming that's what he did."

"If I were a gambling woman, I'd bet money on it. No, this wasn't an accident. It's certainly a suspicious death."

"Which leaves all suspicion pointing to Brenda?"

"If it was the bread that contained the nuts, she will be the prime suspect. Do you think she's capable of murder?"

"I don't know her well enough to say, but from what I've seen of her, she's outgoing, bubbly and kind – complete opposite to Waverley. I wouldn't have thought so, but you're the detective."

Ignoring the goading, Rachel continued, "That's what I thought, so is she just the unwitting scapegoat or is she being framed? Then again, she does have a strong enough motive: that of protecting her sister and nephew from a beast of a man who was probably threatening to do them both harm if his demands weren't met, whatever they were. People have killed for less reason."

"Agreed, but this death would have to have been meticulously pre-planned, surely? I could accept Brenda, or anyone, killing in a moment of madness, but not in such a calculated way. Bread is baked fresh each night, so it would have been prepared hours before it went to his room."

"Unless nut residue was sprinkled on top once he placed an order."

"No, he would have smelled that. Someone with that degree of allergy would see and smell it a mile off, unless it was within the bread itself. Even then, I can't understand why he didn't taste it and spit the bread out, but there's no sign of that. The room seems clean, no vomit."

"Thank you for that detail, Nurse Bradshaw. Do we know for sure that Brenda baked the bread?"

Sarah looked thoughtful. "As far as I'm aware, she prepares or oversees all bread products for those with allergies and sensitivities. The night crew bake the rest."

"I thought you said all the bread was baked at night."

"I meant most of it. Brenda starts work at 5am – that's night to me."

"Well if it does turn out to be the bread, and that's the most likely, Jason could be forced to arrest her as all the evidence points to her. But there could still be others in the frame for this if it is murder."

"Such as?"

"Anyone who hated him enough to go to great lengths to remove the epi-pens from his room prior to ensuring he was fed with something that would cause a catastrophic allergic reaction, resulting in an unpleasant death."

"A cold-blooded killer, then? I still don't know how

they could have tampered with the bread and known he was going to get it, unless it was someone from the bakery, and that takes us back to poor Brenda. It does make more sense that it was premeditated rather than last-minute if the epi-pens were removed, and that would explain why the drawer was open and Stefan was found on the floor."

"I'm afraid it does. If I'm right, and the killer isn't Brenda, they removed the pens, intercepted the bread and swapped it or somehow tampered with it, and then returned the pens after the deed was done, before the body was found. We need to find out who it was as soon as possible, and before Waverley does something stupid. I can't see him staying out of the investigation for long.

"It won't be easy to find the culprit because your maître d was not well liked, but we need to find out who else had access to the room, and how and at what point the food was tampered with. But for now, Nurse Bradshaw, I think you should get a few hours' beauty sleep, and I'll head back to my room to look through these papers from the safe for a couple of hours before breakfasting in the Club Restaurant. Do you think you could ask Jason to meet up with us this afternoon for tea?"

"Creams?"

Creams patisserie was their favourite haunt for afternoon meet-ups, and the surcharge meant it was less busy than other public areas on board ship.

"Sounds ideal. What about your parents?"

"Mum's having a massage and Dad's going to a talk on the Spanish Civil War, so they'll be out of the way for an hour or so. We're dining in the officers' dining room in the evening. I take it you'll join us?"

"I will if I can. It depends whether I need to do some more digging in the Club Restaurant, and on what Marjorie has to say in the morning."

Sarah raised her eyebrows, but decided not to give Rachel the usual lecture about staying out of trouble, for which Rachel was grateful. They walked back to Sarah's room and Rachel hugged her friend.

"Sleep tight, I'll see you this afternoon."

Sarah yawned again, barely able to keep her eyes open. "See you at three."

Rachel marched along the corridor and ran up the stairs to wake herself up before returning to her stateroom. She made herself a black coffee and sat on the bed while she went through some of the neatly piled and organised papers she'd removed from Sosa's safe. They were mainly letters and documents, along with the photographs. The letters and notes she read made interesting study and added a fresh light to the case.

"What were you up to, Stefan Sosa?"

Some of the photos featured an Englishwoman, who Rachel assumed was Christine Jones. These were in a pile joined together by a blue elastic band. There were four other elastic bands of different colours keeping together separate piles of photos, some of which featured a number of other people yet to be identified.

The images began to blur into one and her eyelids felt heavy. Her tired brain could not take in any further information, so she put the stash of letters and photos in her bedside drawer and mulled over the events of the previous day, her findings in the wallet and the night's exploration into Stefan Sosa's room. She tried to relive the conversation she'd had with him on the bus. Something significant filtered through the fog, but then it was lost as she drifted off into a deep sleep.

# Chapter 8

Rachel awoke with a start at the sound of stateroom attendants clattering trolleys along the corridor outside her room. She looked at her watch: eight-thirty. There was just enough time to shower and change before going for breakfast in the Club Restaurant.

Rubbing sleep out of her eyes, she examined herself in the bathroom mirror. The dark lines underneath her eyes told her just how much sleep she hadn't got over the past forty-eight hours.

"You're mad, Rachel Prince. Why don't you just take a holiday like everyone else?" Her reflection didn't reply and she shook her head before she really did lose the plot.

Twenty minutes later, she was being shown to a window seat in the busy restaurant by Pash, the waiter she had met the night before who appeared to be assuming the maître d role. She tried to see through the friendly facade, noticing the smile plastered on his face didn't reach his eyes, which were sharp, almost cold. That was something he and his deceased boss appeared to have in common. She racked her brains, trying to recall what had come to her when she was drifting off to sleep. There had been angry, flashing eyes, but nothing else.

Pash was waiting for her to answer a question she clearly hadn't heard.

"Still no sign of Mr Sosa?" She gazed innocently up at him once seated and didn't miss the brief flicker of fear, nor the hesitation in his voice.

"It seems our maître d has taken ill and won't be working in this restaurant any longer. I have been put in charge now, madam." His puffed-out chest told her all she needed to know about the ambitious young senior waiter.

"Congratulations on your promotion, although I expect you would rather have your old boss well again. That's sad he's ill, I was speaking with him on the bus yesterday. He seemed to have a lot on his mind, poor man – he said as much."

Pash's eyes widened, making them look like saucers in his otherwise thin face.

"What sort of things?"

Ignoring the question struck her as the best thing to do. "I do hope he will feel better soon, I wonder if I should send him a card."

"I'm not sure if that's possible, madam, although it's very kind of you." His painted smile didn't even turn up the corners of his mouth this time. She had clearly rattled him.

"Never mind, perhaps I'll ask Sarah Bradshaw if she

can pass on my good wishes. She's a friend of mine. I was with her last night at dinner."

"Oh yes," he stuttered. "Now I remember. I'm sorry, madam, I had better see the next guests in." He gestured to another waiter to come over. "Sash will be your waiter this morning. Enjoy your breakfast, madam."

The facade was back in place as Pash strolled elegantly towards the desk where people paused before being shown to their seats. But there was no denying his stiffness and sudden change in manner, despite a half-hearted attempt at concealment. That could just be embarrassment at not wanting to tell her that the man she had met the previous day had died – it would hardly be a good advertisement for the restaurant, but there could be some other reason. Perhaps she would find her answers in the late Sosa's meticulous notes.

"Tea, miss?"

Another waiter had appeared, his badge revealing Sacha to be his name and his home country Russia. He was awaiting her answer.

"Coffee, please."

Sacha returned a few minutes later with a pot of coffee and began pouring.

"I see you're from Russia. Have you worked on the *Coral Queen* long?"

"This is my second tour, miss. My sister works on board, she got me the job. Is this your first cruise?"

"No, I've been on this ship a few times before. It's a

lovely vessel. I like the people and find the staff friendly, especially restaurant staff. You seem to have a friendly bunch in here."

For the second time in as many minutes, she noticed another look of hesitation as he steeled himself to reply.

"We do our best to be friendly, ma'am. Are you travelling alone?" He got over his hesitation quickly, and the flirtatious upturn of his mouth and the depth of his almost black eyes gave off pheromones in abundance. Although the beautiful Rachel was used to men flirting with her, the crew on board the *Coral Queen* usually behaved more circumspectly.

"Yes and no. My fiancé is working over Christmas so I'm taking the opportunity to meet up with my friend, Sarah Bradshaw. You may have met her – she's a nurse on board and her boyfriend is Jason Goodridge."

Sacha looked as if she had hit him in the chest at the mention of Jason, but he managed to control himself, absentmindedly straightening his jacket.

"I do know Nurse Bradshaw, she is well liked on board. I will send over Mishka to take your breakfast order, miss."

*At this rate I'll have met the whole restaurant staff in one sitting.* They certainly were twitchy, but that might be understandable – they had after all just heard of the death of their manager. Her antenna piqued by the responses she had drawn so far, she decided it wouldn't hurt to continue probing.

Rachel looked around to see Sacha whispering something to Mishka, and Pash was avoiding eye contact with her.

*I'm clearly not going to be the most popular guest in this restaurant, but I'm used to it.*

Mishka came to take her order and avoided any attempt at conversation, giving nothing away other than what his badge revealed: his name was Mishka and he was also from Russia. A short, plump man with dark bags beneath his sky-blue eyes, he had fair hair tied back in a ponytail and had clearly been warned off by Sacha. It was obviously the Jason link that had rattled them, but why? Jason was amicable and the waiters had seemed friendly enough with him the night before. Their reactions made her all the more suspicious that one of them might have deliberately caused the death of their boss.

When Mishka brought her food, she opted for the blunt approach. He wasn't allowed to be rude to a guest, so why not?

"Mishka, I hear the maître d I met on the bus coming down yesterday has been taken ill. Do you know how I might get a message to him?"

Mishka's serving hand took on a tremor. "I'm sorry, miss, I don't know. We don't socialise after work."

"Really? I'd have thought you'd enjoy socialising after your long, hard days. My friend, Sarah Bradshaw, says that restaurant staff often have get-togethers."

"Not with our seniors, miss, and certainly not with

Stefan Sosa." He couldn't hide his dislike of the maître d; finally she felt she was getting somewhere.

"I did hear he's a hard taskmaster and, to be honest, when I met him, he seemed an unhappy man. Perhaps he was feeling ill."

"No, he was always like that. A miserable man and rotten to the core."

"Was, did you say? Oh dear, has something serious happened?"

"Sorry, I shouldn't have said that, but if you are friends with nurse, you will find out anyway. Stefan Sosa died yesterday."

"I'm so sorry, that must be most upsetting."

"Don't be sorry, none of us are. If you knew him like we did, you wouldn't be sorry either."

"Mishka!" Pash stood behind him. "Other guests are waiting."

"Sorry, it was my fault, I kept him talking."

"Some things are best not talked about. You will excuse me." Pash huffed and turned on his heels. His brusque response didn't give Rachel confidence that, when it came to it, he would be any more forgiving than his previous boss.

*Well that put me in my place,* she thought. There was no doubt that Stefan had been right when he'd told her the crew hated him, and not without reason from the information she had gathered so far, but what had he done to cause such vehement anger? Okay, he was a cruel man if one was married to him. But domestic violence usually confined itself to the home, and in her experience was often well covered up by the perpetrator. This man seemed to have managed to draw such angst that even after his death, people were dispensing with the politeness loss of life generally elicited.

*There must be someone who liked him or was close to him, surely?* She was certain that when she read the rest of Sosa's notes and letters, she would be closer to discovering what this team of seemingly harmless waiting staff was hiding.

Towards the end of breakfast, Rachel observed a freshly groomed and immaculately dressed Jason speaking to Pash, who nodded grimly. If she hadn't known Jason had been on a nightshift, she would never have suspected it. He handed Pash a list before strolling through the restaurant towards one of the waiters working down the far end. The man followed Jason out of the restaurant.

Jason caught her eye, but didn't openly acknowledge her. He was obviously starting his interviews of restaurant staff; she would be keen to hear what he uncovered later, but for now she had some of her own digging to do.

Deciding it was time to leave, she walked casually out of the restaurant and headed to her room to read the rest of the notes and study the photos. Then she could take a well-earned nap.

The investigation and nap would have to wait, she realised as she found Waverley hovering outside her room for the second time in as many days. He was in uniform so at least he was still the chief of security, but as she looked at his pale, drawn expression, she realised he only had one thing on his mind: the Brenda and Stefan Sosa connection.

"May I speak with you?" he blurted out before there was any opportunity for polite greeting.

"Yes, of course. Please come in."

Once inside her room, he appeared to gather himself and became more like the Waverley she had got to know and appreciate: professional and together, if a little abrupt sometimes.

"I need to see the note."

She was about to ask what note, fearing Sarah had given away details of their night-time incursion into Sosa's room, but that wasn't it. She could tell from the look in Waverley's eyes that Jason had reneged on their agreement and told his boss about the note from Brenda. She sighed and pulled it out of the wallet in her handbag.

"I asked Jason not to tell you until we'd had the opportunity to delve a little deeper. I didn't want this to upset you."

He nodded as he read it and handed it back to her. "I understand your reasoning, but please don't try to protect me. It might do more harm than good. I need to know what is happening. Goodridge understands that; he's agreed to share information, even though I realise I'm putting him in an impossible situation." He coughed and brushed the imaginary hair from the top of his head. The receding hairline seemed to have worsened overnight.

"Are you asking me to get involved in an investigation, Chief Waverley?"

Waverley grimaced. "Don't toy with me, Rachel. I know you're already involving yourself, but yes, that is what I'm asking. I don't need to explain how important this is to me – my wife is innocent."

"Okay, I'll agree as long as you agree not to put yourself in a position where you could lose your job. You know why the captain has removed you from the investigation – you're too close to it."

"Yes, I realise that, but I'll go mad with worry if I don't know what's going on. Brenda swore to me last night that she had nothing to do with this. That's good enough for me, so you and Goodridge need to find out who did it, if it wasn't an accident."

"Is there any news from the post-mortem?"

"The coroner believes Dr Bentley's initial diagnosis is the correct one, but will not be carrying out a post-mortem until this evening or tomorrow morning. It seems he has a backlog." Waverley's eyebrows almost hit the ceiling. "We'll hear back on the likely cause of the fatal reaction as soon as the PM is concluded. Nothing else to do at present but assume the allergen got into the bread by mistake or by design and brought about an anaphylactic reaction."

Rachel took a deep breath. "How is Brenda taking it?"

"I can't honestly say. She's devastated that she may have made a mistake and blame could be attributed to her or one of her assistants, but she's relieved in a way that Sosa is no longer a threat to her sister or her nephew. It's been a difficult time for them all. At least Christine will have a good Christmas, although I expect she'll be worried sick about Brenda."

Rachel nodded. "Will her son be joining her for Christmas?"

"He's staying with friends in Exeter for parties and what not before travelling up to London on Christmas Eve. He's as relieved as his mother is from what I can gather. Brenda spoke to Christine this morning." Waverley was being brutally honest, but things were not looking good for Brenda as they stood.

"I'll do what I can," she said as she escorted Waverley to the door. "Just one thing – did you move the pens around in Sosa's drawer?"

"No, why?"

"I'm not sure yet, let me think about it."

Waverley shrugged. She watched him walk away along the corridor, grateful he hadn't registered she might have been in the dead man's room. His step was purposeful, but lacked the usual confidence.

"Don't worry, chief," she called, "we'll find out who did it."

# Chapter 9

As soon as Waverley left, the telephone in Rachel's room rang. Feeling like she might never sleep again, she picked it up.

"Hello,"

"Rachel, I'm so pleased to find you in, I've been calling all morning."

Jolting herself back to life, she remembered the message from the previous evening.

"Marjorie! I'm so sorry, I forgot you were going to call this morning. I've not long got back from breakfast."

"That's alright, dear. I'm sorry to bother you when you're on holiday, but a crisis might be brewing."

Marjorie was not generally prone to exaggeration. Rachel was now on full alert.

"Tell me what it is and how you think I can help."

"Do you remember a month ago I said I'd given Carlos's telephone number to some friends of mine?"

"Yes I do, but Carlos never heard from them."

"No, fools that they were, they decided to hire someone else. That was their prerogative, but I'm sure if they had hired dear Carlos, we wouldn't be having this conversation now."

Rachel heard the tension as Marjorie's voice squeaked. "Perhaps you should just tell me what's going on."

"Quite. Well, my dear old friends Felicity and Aaron McCauley came to see me last month. Throughout the evening, I could tell there was something bothering them. I asked them about it and they didn't want to say at first, but after a few glasses of port, Aaron loosened up and out came an intriguing story."

Lady Marjorie chuckled. Her mischievous streak was something Rachel loved about her dear elderly friend.

"It turns out they believe their elder son, who divorced a year ago, has married a gold digger on the rebound. He married again just a few months after the divorce went through. They are extremely wealthy – I'm positively poor by comparison – and as their son, Harry, will inherit the controlling interest in a successful company at the cutting edge – so I am told – of AI innovation – I assume you know about AI?"

"Artificial intelligence, yes I'm aware of the term and of its significance for growth in the future. Carlos tells me we'll all have a personal robot by the time he and I reach forty. Personally, I can't wait."

"Well hopefully I will be with my late husband by then. Or perhaps I'll be in my dotage and a robot will be a trusty companion. Anyway, I'm not sure what type of AI their company is involved in because much of it is top secret, but they are extremely concerned about this woman as far as I could tell."

"What makes them think she is a gold digger?"

"They didn't go into too many details, but Aaron felt that she had targeted their son and rushed him into marriage. They warned and advised him to request she sign a prenuptial agreement, but he adamantly refused, despite forking out a small fortune to his first wife."

"Okay, so their son may have made the wrong marriage choice, but why does that put your friends in danger?"

"Felicity and Aaron have noticed that Harry is losing weight. He falls asleep a lot, even when at work, and is complaining of indigestion. He visits them every night on his way home from the office to chat about the business and catch up. They say he puts on a show of pretending all is well in the marriage and they are reluctant to probe as they don't wish to alienate him. To cut down a very detailed conversation, they believe that Louise – the wife – is having an affair and that she might be slowly poisoning their son."

"That is a serious allegation. I assume they hired the private investigator to follow the wife or dig up some dirt on her?"

"I'm afraid that's about the sum of it. They wouldn't be away from home now if it weren't for an anniversary celebration. They are on board the *Coral Queen* along with Harry and Louise, and here is where it gets worse."

Rachel found herself holding her breath. "You think

that the wife – Louise, did you say? – is planning to get rid of your friends and take out Harry by poison at a later date?"

"I know so."

"You'd better tell me the rest." Rachel felt a headache coming on.

"The silly private investigator they hired managed to lose sight of the woman. You see, she wasn't supposed to be on the cruise because it had been booked and planned when Harry was still going through the divorce. The family decided that a Christmas cruise would be just the thing for their parents' Golden Wedding anniversary. The younger son, who has his own business, offered to take care of their business while they were away, feeling it would help take Harry's mind off the divorce, but after all this had been arranged, Harry remarried. Louise agreed she didn't really want to be a part of the celebrations, Felicity and Aaron think in part because she knew they had reservations about her. Harry may even have told her about the prenup idea."

"But now you've found out she's on board."

"Yes, after the investigator lost her, his checks revealed that she had bought a last-minute ticket to join her husband on the cruise. He gained access to Louise's office – she works in the same company as her husband – and found television recordings on DVDs locked away in her drawers covering suicides and misadventures at sea. Not only that, but the PI has discovered newspaper cuttings of accidents occurring on board cruise ships where people go overboard and are never seen again. On top of that, there was a book on poisons in her bedside drawer."

"Was there anything on her computer?"

"No, this PI says she's too clever for that. She would know that there might be an investigation if Harry's parents were to die and it turned out they had spoken to their friends or to Gary, their younger son, about her."

"Why would she leave a clear paper trail, though?"

"That's not clear, but it appears she made a hasty departure, so perhaps she was planning to destroy the evidence on her return. As you know, deleted files on computers are not as easy to get rid of as they can be recovered from the hard drive.

"The PI believes that Louise has two reasons to be on board the *Coral Queen*. Firstly to continue lacing Harry's drinks or food with a poison – as yet unknown – and secondly to kill the McCauleys and get her hands on the inheritance as soon as possible."

"As you say, it's all very last-minute. What brought about the suddenness of this scheme?"

"The PI believes opportunity, and also his surveillance has revealed arguments in the marriage. Perhaps she thinks another divorce might be brewing, or maybe she just can't wait. There is another man she meets regularly when Harry is at work – she herself only works three days a week. The PI did a bit of digging and found out from a receptionist at the health club where they meet that she has apparently been seeing him for three years. This relationship has been hidden, but has continued since she married. He works for a competing AI firm and is possibly the real brains behind the operation. He's well placed to move over and take on management of the McCauleys company. I suspect that he will marry the woman shortly after Harry dies."

"That's awful. Why did the PI come to you?"

"He hasn't been able to contact the McCauleys as they left their mobile phones at home and they had given him my contact details in case he found something significant while they were away. He didn't want to contact the purser's office for fear of alerting Louise."

"How low people can be. I believe you of course, Marjorie, but this is all circumstantial. She could have a fascination for suicide or marine accidents, and her husband might have some underlying health problem. What would you like me to do?"

"Rachel, you've done it before. I would like you to prevent a murder."

# Chapter 10

The ship was buzzing with excited passengers enjoying their Christmas break as Rachel made her way towards Creams, feeling refreshed after sleeping for most of the time since her telephone call with Marjorie. She eyed the Christmas tree standing in all its glory in the atrium and the flocks of people exploring what was the main hub of the ship during the daytime.

*If only we can get this crime solved as quickly as possible, I can have some chill time.*

Work had been demanding since she'd become a detective constable and was likely to bring many more challenges when she got a DS post. There were few vacancies in London so she and Carlos had agreed that she should apply to areas elsewhere as he travelled the country anyway, but she wasn't keen to give up the luxurious flat Marjorie had invited her to inhabit in Knightsbridge, an area she truly loved.

Nevertheless, it was looking more and more clear that the only way to get promotion was to move. There were numerous vacancies in the Midlands, so she had sent away applications and copies of her CV before leaving for the cruise.

"You look like you've got the world's troubles on your shoulders." Sarah arrived behind Rachel and put her arm around her.

"I was just thinking about jobs and what might be next for me. I think I'll end up in the Midlands."

"I remember that case you solved when you were at uni, wasn't that in the Midlands? Gory business – are you likely to end up in Leicester?"

Rachel smiled. "I've been wondering that myself. I don't think DI Bond would be pleased if I ended up there and I certainly wouldn't be keen to work for her, but who knows? Anyway, perhaps this case will keep me out of trouble and stop me worrying about the future."

"That's not like you to worry about the future. Your faith will keep you going whatever happens, it always does. You do still have a job, after all."

Rachel nodded. "You're right, it's all in hand, but I'd still like to know where I'm going. I want to be a proper detective."

They both laughed as they found a table hidden in the corner of the quiet patisserie where they would be able to speak without being overheard. Rachel looked round the room. There were just a handful of guests occupying tables nearer to the windows in the main area of the café.

Sarah glanced through the menu and Rachel felt guilty as her friend looked tired.

"How was surgery this morning?"

"Relatively quiet considering it's winter and there're a lot of coughs and colds going round already. The trouble is people bring them on board, and then the viruses spread rapidly as they congregate in the busy passenger hubs."

"Not to mention through the air conditioning, or should I say heating system at this time of year?"

"That too, but at least so far it appears to be a relatively mild virus. We don't want any flu going round, even if some people are convinced they've got the flu when they have a cold."

"Yes, we get that a lot at work. People always say they've got the flu, and then miraculously recover within a few days. My understanding of flu is that it lasts for longer than that and usually knocks people off their feet."

"Oh, here's Jason."

Both women looked up. Rachel loved the way Sarah's eyes lit up whenever Jason entered a room and wondered if her own did the same when she saw Carlos. She suspected they did; she definitely still got flutters when she saw her fiancé.

Jason joined them at the table, clearly resisting the temptation to kiss Sarah in a passenger area, but the affection in his eyes said it all.

"Hello, you two. How has your day been?"

Sarah repeated the news she had just given Rachel about a relatively quiet surgery and coughs and colds. "Brigitte's on call now and I'm on tonight after we've had dinner with my parents. I take it you're still coming?"

Jason nodded before looking at Rachel and giving her time to respond to his initial question.

"Mine is a lot better now I've had a sleep. I forget how tiring nightshifts are when you stop them." She didn't mention breakfast as Jason knew she had been in the Club Restaurant earlier in the day. He too looked tired. "It looks like you haven't been to bed yet, though."

He looked sheepishly towards Sarah, who was about to scold him. "Sorry, not yet. It's been full on, but I'm going to grab a couple of hours when we're finished here so I'll be fresh for tonight, don't worry." He looked up as one of the waiters appeared. "Cream scones with all the trimmings and a cappuccino, please, Henri."

"Yes, sir. Ladies?"

"I'll have a blueberry muffin and tea, please," Sarah answered.

"Coffee and cheesecake for me."

The waiter went away to gather their orders together and they chatted amicably until he returned. Once the food and drink was in front of them, Jason coughed to bring them to attention.

"You sounded just like Waverley then," laughed Rachel.

Jason laughed too. "They say you get like the people you work with."

"Don't you dare! I like you just as you are. Waverley's fine, but he's not Jason Goodridge." Sarah beamed at him.

"Don't worry, I'm still here." He gazed at the adoring eyes looking at him across the table.

"Er hum, if you two love birds could concentrate for a while, we have an investigation to discuss."

Jason pulled himself away from the eye-lock and moved his empty plate, having stuffed two scones down in a matter of minutes while still managing to flirt with Sarah. Rachel suspected he hadn't had time to eat all day. He removed a tablet from a document holder that he had placed on the floor when he came in.

"Okay, Rachel, first tell us what you found out in the restaurant this morning."

Rachel relayed her conversations with Pash, Sacha and Mishka and their behaviour. "I think Mishka would have said a lot more, but Pash was hanging around and called him away. In fact, Pash was decidedly twitchy when I mentioned I knew you and Sarah."

"Yes, I was hoping he wouldn't catch on to that, but as we'd already eaten in there last night, I'm sure he would have remembered sooner rather than later. He's friendly enough most of the time and polite, but he does seem to have issues with authority. It could be as simple as that."

"No wonder he didn't like his ex-boss, there was no-one more authoritarian than Sosa," said Sarah.

Jason looked down at the tablet and pulled up his interview notes. "He says he was in the restaurant at the time of Sosa's death. Claudia Kitova and the galley records confirm that the meal was delivered at 5pm. The waiters didn't go on duty until 5.30pm so we do have a half-hour gap in all their alibis, which doesn't help. We have to assume that the food was replaced or intercepted between 4.45pm and 5pm. Claudia had two trays to deliver, the first to a passenger on the next floor up. She left Sosa's tray on a trolley in the crew-only room on that floor for no more than five minutes. We assume that if there was interference, it happened at that time or when the bread was waiting for the hot food to be added to the tray in the galley." He pulled out the galley delivery log. "That gap is a little longer, around ten minutes."

"Was Brenda there all that time?"

"No, by chance or by design, I can't confirm which, she left the galley to attend to a cut finger as per health and safety rules. She had to locate a finger dressing from the first aid box."

"What do you mean, by design?" asked Sarah, open-mouthed. "You can't think she would tamper with the bread."

"I'm trying not to think anything; I have to investigate objectively. Waverley told me just as much this morning. He says I have to follow procedure to the letter."

"Including keeping him up-to-date against the express instructions of your captain, you mean?" Rachel teased. "Thanks for telling him about the Brenda note."

"Sorry." He looked down at the table.

Sarah nudged Rachel. "It seems I'm out of the loop here. You mean Jason told Waverley?" Turning to him, "You promised!"

"I did no such thing. Anyway, the boss looked so distraught this morning and desperately wanted to be kept informed. If I hadn't told him, we would have lost trust, and trust is everything in this job. Rachel understands that."

Rachel smiled and nodded. "I do, and on that note, Sarah and I have a confession to make, but for now, go on. What else did Pash have to say?"

Jason winked meekly at Sarah, checking she understood why he'd broken confidence. Seemingly satisfied that her grin confirmed she did, he continued.

"At first he was evasive, trying to pretend he liked his boss, but once I got firm and told him if he was lying to me it would look bad and his chances of promotion would be out the window, he became more forthcoming. He confirmed he didn't like Stefan Sosa, saying that none of the waiters did. The boss nit-picked everything they did, always looking out for mistakes and embarrassing them in front of passengers. He says the staff were always nervous around Sosa and that made them clumsy. Two waiters had managed to get transfers up to the buffet so there were two new starters on boarding day – I've discounted them from the investigation. He also said that he always arrived early at the restaurant, before Sosa, so that he wouldn't be accused of slacking. He swears he was there at 5pm."

"Can anyone confirm that?" asked Rachel.

"No, the others don't arrive until 5.30ish, but they confirm that Pash was there before them and that he is always early to work. Mishka Prostakov and Sacha Voronin said they hated their boss, but not enough to want him dead. They seemed to think Sosa had something over the wine waitress, Danielle. She insists there was nothing and the others were just jealous, and that she got on well with the man. She wouldn't budge, even when I told her if there had been something, she could tell me now and that he could no longer do her any harm. She blamed Pash for her boss's behaviour. According to her, Pash was after the top job and went out of his way to make the others dislike Sosa, frequently sabotaging the smooth running of the restaurant."

"My, my, a nest of vipers by the sounds of it," said Rachel thoughtfully. "Do you think there's any truth in what the two men say? We do know he was violent towards women. Perhaps Danielle was afraid of him."

"There's more to it than that, I think, otherwise she would tell me now."

"It's not always that easy to admit to, and we can't rule her out of the equation." Jason nodded. "What about their backgrounds?" Rachel quizzed.

"Nothing untoward. They are all who they say they are, no criminal records came up in their pre-employment checks. Danielle Barcellos has a daughter who lives with her mother in Portugal. It seems she got pregnant on board ship a few years before my time; the child is now seven years old."

Rachel straightened up immediately. "How long has Sosa been working on this ship?"

"Twelve years – I see what you're getting at. You think he might be the father. There's no way of knowing that, unless Danielle admits to it."

"I could check her medical records to see if the father was named at the time of the pregnancy," suggested Sarah. "It will be on file, but unless it's relevant to the investigation, I don't think we will be able to breach confidentiality."

"We'll hold fire on that one. Perhaps you could ask her socially?"

"I don't really know her, but Bernard knows everyone, so he might already be in the loop. He would have been on board at that time. I'll ask him."

"I assume you believe the kitchen maid, Claudia Kitova?" asked Rachel.

"Yes I do, she's a hard-working galley attendant, been with the cruise line for ten years on and off. Brenda is adamant she would have neither the will nor the brains to tamper with food in this way. Here's where the plot thickens, though—"

Rachel and Sarah shifted in their seats, eyes focussed on Jason.

"I've been through the passenger manifest and it

seems there are guests on board that were known to Sosa."

"Now that is interesting. Who?" asked Rachel.

"His sister and brother-in-law joined the ship yesterday."

"That is a little too coincidental. Have you interviewed them?"

"No, we didn't know they were on board until we went through an address book that was retrieved from Sosa's room this morning. It was chance, really. I asked Ravanos to throw all the names in the address book through our computer to see if there were any passenger matches, and was as surprised as anyone to find there were."

Rachel and Sarah exchanged glances.

"What aren't you two telling me? Why do I think you already knew about the address book?"

"Sorry, that's part of the confession, but go on for now," Rachel encouraged.

"Their names are Stella and Paulo Gonzalez and they seemingly don't even know Sosa's dead yet. I'm waiting to see if they go to guest services and ask about him. If they don't, that would seem very suspicious, wouldn't it?"

"That's not very kind. What if they have nothing to do with this? They have a right to know, Jason."

Jason looked at Sarah. "I'm sorry, love, but I think it's odd they haven't already made enquiries. I promise if they haven't by tomorrow morning, I'll ask Dr Bentley to see them."

Jason turned to Rachel. Anticipating what he was going to say, she prompted him.

"There's more, isn't there?"

He grimaced, clearly still smarting from Sarah's rebuke. "Brenda and Christine's father is on board."

Rachel groaned. "You think he might have come to seek revenge on behalf of his daughter? Does Brenda know?"

"She does now; she's terrified he might be involved. It's a complete and utter mess, but I don't know how it could have been a passenger. They would have needed to know that Sosa had ordered food."

"And if my theory is correct, they would have had to move the epi-pens before he ate and replace them afterwards. I take it you didn't move the pens?"

"No, Waverley was there first. I didn't look in the drawer. But how do you know about the pens and why do you think they were moved?"

"I'm coming to that. You're right, though. I think we should stay focussed on the crew for now." Rachel wasn't sure at all, but they had to start somewhere and the suspect list was growing out of control.

"I agree, but I would suggest you try to befriend the couple and Brenda's father just in case."

"How am I supposed to do that?"

"How you always do it, Rachel – with that innate charm that comes with being a vicar's daughter." Sarah laughed.

"You could have put that a bit nicer!" Rachel quipped back.

"Now, now, ladies, I hope I'm not going to have to separate you two." Jason joined in with their banter. Rachel and Sarah couldn't be closer, they were best friends forever.

Sarah thumped his arm. "I'd like to see you try."

"Are you happy to keep up with eating in the Club Restaurant, Rachel?" Jason asked.

"You can take Mum and Dad with you tomorrow," added Sarah. "That will give you a cover. I'm taking them for dinner with the officers tonight. You two are invited, but we can do the same again in a few days' time, which means Jason can get some proper sleep."

"Okay, I can do that. In fact, it would be my pleasure." Rachel had known the Bradshaws most of her life, growing up in the same village. They attended the church where her father presided, and she and Sarah had been at school together before going to the same university in Leeds and later sharing a flat. "For tonight, though, I will just head up to the buffet, have a quick meal and an early night. Lack of sleep has caught up on me."

"Shall we meet up in the Jazz Bar tomorrow night around nine?" suggested Sarah.

"Sounds good to me," said Jason. "But before I go, what about this confession?"

"I'm not being evasive, but can I tell you tomorrow? You've likely guessed right – we went to take a look in Sosa's room in the early hours. My fault, not Sarah's. I found some notes and photos, but have only managed to skim through the first few as Waverley accosted me after breakfast, and I've slept on and off ever since. I'll go and check through them now and hand them over tomorrow, unless I find anything urgent. Is that okay with you?"

"That's fine, I trust you. Now I too need to go get some sleep."

"Me three before evening surgery," agreed Sarah. "I'll meet you in the Jazz Bar tomorrow, Rachel. If I'm late, you'll know I've been called to attend someone."

They left Creams together and Rachel discretely left the couple to walk away to say their goodbyes in private. She kicked herself for forgetting to mention Marjorie's concerns about the McCauleys, but Jason was clearly tired and had reached his limit for today. As had she. There was always tomorrow.

# Chapter 11

The day had flown past with activities she'd booked prior to the cruise to keep her occupied on sea days. She had avoided the Club Restaurant throughout the day to give her brain a rest, and to lull the staff working there into feeling secure. But Rachel and the Bradshaws were in there now, enjoying a pleasant evening meal.

Mary Bradshaw chatted to Rachel like she was a second daughter and cajoled her into eating more than she would have liked to. There had been little opportunity to speak to any of the waiters in any respect, other than when they were ordering food, as the restaurant was heaving. Passengers had obviously discovered the haven and were flocking in. Pash told them they would need to book in early if they wished to eat there after today. He said it with a smile, but Rachel detected a slight irritation whenever he looked at her. In his eyes, she was clearly Jason's spy, so he had good reason to avoid her.

Then again, if he had nothing to hide, he wouldn't need to. When people behaved suspiciously, there was always something going on, experience told her, and the more he kept her at arm's length, the more she determined to find out what it was.

"Rachel, you're miles away again," Mary chided. "You were just the same as a child, always thinking about something else, and now I expect you're missing your Carlos."

Rachel sat bolt upright, feeling guilty on both counts. Yes, she had been miles away, but no, she wasn't thinking about Carlos.

*Poor Carlos, how does he put up with me?* "Sorry."

"That's alright, dear. I was just asking if you were ready. Gilbert and I are going to the show."

Rachel finished the dregs of the after-dinner coffee she was drinking and picked up her handbag. "I'm ready."

"Tell Sarah we'll see her at 10am tomorrow, would you? She's got the whole day off."

"I will, does she know where?"

"You've forgotten, haven't you? Really, Rachel! We arrive in Lisbon tomorrow and have booked on the tour to Fátima. You're coming too, unless your amnesia gets any worse. I'm beginning to worry about you. Are you sure everything is alright?"

"Yes of course. Sorry, I only finished nights the day before yesterday. Not quite with it yet." She smiled sheepishly and Gilbert winked to let her know he understood.

The Bradshaws kissed her on the cheek and she left

them to book a table for an early breakfast while she made her way towards the Jazz Bar. The public areas were busy with people heading towards the Coral Restaurant for dinner or to the theatre. It was too early for her meeting with Sarah and Jason, but she might as well find a table and order a drink while she waited.

At this time in the evening, the majority of passengers were in either of the main hubs, so the Jazz Bar was a little less busy. A barman who recognised her from previous sailings nodded an acknowledgement. Rachel found a booth away from the main jazz band, which afforded a little more privacy than the other parts of the bar. Having settled in, she people-watched while waiting for the others, a hobby of hers and one that was useful in the day job.

Another barman brought her a martini and lemonade.

"I haven't ordered yet, how did you know?"

"I was told to bring it to you, miss."

"Surprise!" Bernard jumped up from behind the high seat where she was sitting. He placed a beer on the table and sat opposite, grinning from ear to ear.

"Thank you, Bernard. It's lovely to see you." She liked the mischievous Filipino nurse.

"Sarah said to tell you she'll be along soon. She's just finishing up with a lady who cut her shin. I expect she drank too much, you know how it is. How is the most beautiful passenger on board the *Coral Queen*?"

"I don't know, I haven't seen her," she bantered back.

They both laughed. Bernard was one of the few men who complimented her beauty without any ulterior motive so she didn't retort with her usual caustic responses when he brought the subject up.

"Ha, got me. It's good to have you on board, Rachel. Things are always so much more interesting when you're around."

"I really don't know what you're talking about."

He was about to explain, but saw the twinkle in her eye. "Got me again."

"It's time you stopped allowing people to die on your watch, if you ask me."

"Ooh, now that hurts. If you don't behave, I won't tell you what I found out."

Rachel straightened up and lowered her voice. "Now you've got me. Is it something to do with Stefan Sosa?"

He beamed, but before he got to tell her, Jason arrived, followed almost immediately by Sarah. Jason's gaze was alert; he had shaved away the shadow from the day before and now cut a handsome figure in his freshly pressed uniform. He sat next to Rachel while Sarah joined Bernard on the bench opposite. Sarah also appeared to have caught up enough on her sleep to present herself in a favourable light – at least from where Rachel was sitting.

"Sorry we're late, I had to see to a passenger and Jason had to convince Waverley to stay away from us."

Rachel gave Jason a sympathetic glance. "It can't be

easy for him when he's usually running the show, and now things are personal."

Jason let out a deep breath. "I can't say I'm finding the situation easy either, I want him to be back in charge."

Rachel believed him. She knew of Jason's loyalty to his boss and the respect he had for Waverley; it was a difficult scenario all round and a bit surreal. This time she was investigating with the chief's permission, not something he would usually have entertained. They needed to get to the bottom of this case.

"Anything more from the coroner?" she asked.

"Just what we knew already, but Waverley's getting frustrated that the PM hasn't been done yet, two days after the event. The coroner doesn't seem to be in any rush, thinks it's a clear-cut case. If it is, he will most likely recommend health and safety procedures are tightened up. Usually I would be pleased, but with the finger pointing at a mistake by Brenda, it's not looking good, and it's only a matter of time before her link to the dead man is discovered outside our small circle and we have to submit the evidence. Then it's more likely to be a murder investigation. Captain Jenson's giving Brenda the benefit of the doubt, but I don't know what he'll do if he finds out about the note."

"It is already looking like murder," said Rachel.

"Yes, but no-one else knows that yet, not even the crew."

"Well that might work in our favour because the killer

will think they are off the hook and will be happy for the kitchen staff to take the blame for an apparent accident."

"Does anyone want to know what I found out?" asked Bernard.

All eyes moved towards the small man with the jolly face. Jason raised his eyebrows, encouraging him to speak.

"Enlighten us."

"I managed to have a chat with Danielle, the wine waitress. I know her from the crew bar where I hang out sometimes, mainly to keep an eye on their drinking and behaviour. I try to work out which of them is likely to get the sack or end up in the medical centre."

Alcohol intake by crew was a cause for concern as many of them would take their free time to extremes. 'Work hard, play hard' was how they excused the behaviour, but it could lead to fights, unprotected sex and alcohol addiction. The medical team did their best to encourage fun while explaining the dangers of excess, but they were fighting a losing battle when it came to the crew bars where the young enjoyed freedom and a bit of spending money for perhaps the first time in their lives. The older crew members also drank heavily at times, some of them behaving like predators, taking advantage of the inebriated youngsters, while others were more like parents protecting the young.

"I found her this afternoon by the crew pool. It was freezing out there so there was no-one else around. Sarah asked me to chat to her, but this was an unexpected encounter."

Rachel wondered what Bernard had been doing out there, but Sarah got the question in first.

"Why were you out there, then?"

"I like to get some fresh air away from passengers sometimes and it's one of the few areas where I can take a brisk walk without having to be polite. Anyway, she was sitting on a poolside chair in the pouring rain, drenched. The pool has been drained for the winter, but the hot tubs are still in use so some of the crew mess around in them, but not today. I warned her she would catch a chill and reminded her she had not had a flu jab yet."

"Bernard's our secret weapon when it comes to flu vaccine non-responders," explained Sarah. "He knows everyone and has the memory of an elephant."

Bernard smiled at the compliment. "Anyway, she said she hadn't got round to it and would come along to morning surgery tomorrow to see me. I've booked her in." He beamed while Jason shuffled, impatient to find out what Bernard had to tell them. "Then she explained that the death of Stefan Sosa had surprised her and she asked me what he'd died from. I explained I wasn't able to say and said I was sorry for her, that it must be hard to lose a colleague."

"You mean you didn't come out with some inappropriate joke? That's a first," teased Sarah.

"I can be sensitive sometimes, you know." He stuck

out his chin and continued, "She said she wasn't upset, just surprised, then it slipped out that she had actually been relieved when she'd heard, and finally she started to cry. I gave her my handkerchief, the one with my initials on, and waited patiently for her to carry on."

"Like we are now," said Jason.

"Sorry. To cut down a long story short..."

Rachel smiled. Bernard occasionally got British idioms muddled.

"...soon after she joined the ship, Sosa seduced her when she had drunk too much whisky. He promised her all sorts of favouritism, which never materialised, and they had a brief relationship. I never suspected there was something going on with her back then. When she got pregnant, she wouldn't say who the father was and we all assumed it was one of those one-night-stands and she probably couldn't – or didn't want to – remember. The relationship was kept hush-hush at Sosa's request and ended after he punched her in the stomach one night after a row."

Jason's fists clenched at this point and Sarah gasped, "She could have lost the baby."

"That's why she ended it. She told him that she would report him if he ever came near her again, and she also told him the baby wasn't his, although it was. As soon as the child was born – a girl, delivered in her hometown in Portugal – she decided that in order to protect herself and her daughter, she would be better off leaving the child with her mother. Later she rejoined the *Coral* and has been sending money home ever since. But around six months ago – she explained – Sosa had started to threaten her with DNA tests and told her he had a right to see his only child."

"Horrible man!" Rachel exclaimed. "I suppose he neglected to tell her he already had a son."

"He kept the ex-wife secret and told Danielle that unless she slipped him the odd bottle of wine, he would challenge paternity and request access through a lawyer. Told her he would argue she was an unfit mother. Through fear, she did as he demanded. Afterwards he told her that she was now a thief, and unless she wanted reporting, she was to do his bidding."

"That's evil. I never liked him, but had no idea he was this low. What bidding?" asked Sarah.

"Favours. She had to keep tabs on the waiters and report what they were saying, so she gave him information that she could glean to convince him that she was doing what he demanded. Some things she kept back."

"Did these favours include sex?" Rachel asked, not really wanting to know the answer, but it was necessary for motive.

"No. Apparently he tried to make it part of the deal, but she said she would rather get the sack or throw herself overboard than let him come near her again."

"Good for her," said Sarah.

"It seems he let that one drop, knowing the line had been drawn. I believe her – she is mortified at the crimes she has committed for him and said she was glad to finally get it off her chest. It was her daughter she was protecting, not herself. She even gave me permission to report her."

"You're not going to do anything, are you, Jason?" Sarah pleaded.

Jason thought for a few minutes, scowling into his lemonade glass while clenching and unclenching his fists. Rachel knew the feeling. He was battling between rage against the dreadful man and his conscience. They let him ponder until finally he looked softly at Sarah.

"I will have to have a word with her, but it will be a gentle warning, I promise. She was coerced so I don't feel the need to come down too heavily over this."

Sarah placed her hand thankfully on his.

"But she is now a suspect in a murder investigation," said Rachel quietly.

"Yes, I'm afraid she is," agreed Jason.

"Well I don't believe she did it," said Sarah angrily. "And I hate to say this, but that man got what was coming to him."

"Sarah!" Bernard exclaimed. "That's something I would say, but not you."

"I'm sorry, that was horrible, wasn't it?"

Jason squeezed her hand. "He was a brute, Sarah. We won't be shedding any tears, but we still need to find his killer and clear Brenda's name."

Sarah nodded. "Did Danielle say anything else?"

"No, she was shivering so I took her inside to get warm and left her in the crew café to get something hot to drink."

"Would you like to join me when I speak to her, Bernard? Perhaps that way she might tell us if she did actually hear any suggestion of a murder plot coming from the other waiters. You never know, she might have heard something."

Bernard nodded. "No problem."

"I don't think she's the killer because she wouldn't have told Bernard all this if she was. She'd just be glad to be rid of the man. I expect she's wrestling with guilt about feeling pleased he's dead more than anything else."

"And she will have alienated her colleagues if they suspect she was spying on them, which it sounds like they did from what they told you yesterday morning, Jason," added Rachel.

"Why don't we speak with her in surgery tomorrow morning?" said Bernard. "That way it will be less threatening and I'll be able to see if she's forgiven me for telling you."

With a plan in place, they decided to call it a night. Rachel made her way back to her stateroom feeling angry about what she'd heard. Was there no end to what some people would do to get their own way?

# Chapter 12

Rachel slept in until 8am having gone out like a light as soon as she got to her room the night before. The moment she came to consciousness, the investigation was at the forefront of her brain. She slapped her head at still not having mentioned anything about the McCauleys to Jason or Sarah and wondered if she should call Waverley before going on her trip today.

Deciding against it, she reassured herself that it was unlikely that any harm would come to them while the ship was in port. If there was a plan to murder them, it would be done during sea days, and she suspected that to avoid much of a chance for investigation, it would happen on the return journey after the visit to the Canary Islands. She would gamble that she was right and discuss it with Jason or Waverley well before then.

Having parked that worry, she got ready to meet Sarah and her parents in the main atrium before they went ashore for the tour to Fátima. It wouldn't have been her choice, but Mary Bradshaw was fascinated by spiritual places and Rachel was happy to go anywhere as long as it involved land and hopefully a long walk. She was missing her exercise routine.

Mary and Gilbert Bradshaw were already standing among a crowd waiting for Rachel and Sarah to arrive. Rachel heard running behind her and turned to see Sarah rushing.

"Is something the matter?"

Sarah panted and stooped to catch her breath. "I thought I was late. What time is it?"

"Quarter to ten, we've got fifteen minutes."

"Blast this watch!" Sarah glared at her wrist. "It's gaining time again, I thought it was fixed."

Rachel knew about the watch problems as her friend had mentioned it on the phone a few weeks before the trip. It was an old favourite watch that Sarah clung on to. Rachel also knew that the Bradshaws had purchased a solar charging watch for their daughter for Christmas because they had discussed presents prior to the cruise so as not to overlap. Sarah was a keen advocate of environmentally friendly living as much as she could be and tried hard to reduce her carbon footprint, as did Rachel.

"Well that's it, you're going to be confined to my memory box." Sarah spoke to the watch, much to Rachel's amusement and Mary Bradshaw's horror.

"Sarah, I do wonder about you sometimes." Then, without pausing for breath, "Good to see you made it, Rachel. We weren't sure you would remember, were we, Gilbert?"

"It was never in doubt," answered her husband. "Don't be a tease, Mary."

Rachel wasn't certain it had been teasing, but she laughed anyway. "I'm looking forward to it."

"Let's get going then, people are boarding the coach."

Sarah stuck her tongue out behind her mother's back and Rachel nudged her. "I hope you're not going to be childish today."

"Only if I'm treated like one."

The happy foursome boarded the coach and Sarah turned to wave to Jason, who was checking passengers off the ship through security. He looked up at the right moment and nodded. Security personnel had to concentrate on the cards they were scanning and check the photos of passengers exiting and entering the ship. Rachel noticed the early birds, who had been off as soon as people were allowed to do so, already returning to the ship. Some would probably have lunch and then go ashore again.

She kicked herself to concentrate on where she was as they found seats towards the rear of the coach. She didn't want another lecture from Mary about being elsewhere.

Sarah sat in the aisle seat so that Rachel could look out of the window during the tour. Mary and Gilbert sat behind them as Rachel recognised voices coming from the seats in front and across the aisle. She nudged Sarah and tilted her head.

Sarah rolled her eyes and groaned before whispering,

"Leave it today." There was no way Rachel would do that and her friend knew it, so she raised her eyebrows in a mock 'leave what?' fashion and got a dig in the ribs for her trouble.

Mishka was sitting in the seat in front of Rachel and Sacha in front of Sarah. Danielle, who had either missed her appointment with Bernard, and therefore with Jason, or been to surgery earlier, was sitting across the aisle from the men, next to someone Rachel couldn't see without craning her neck, but it was a woman, not a man. Pash wasn't there.

The coach left the dockside, and soon afterwards the tour guide introduced herself and began a short history of Lisbon, pointing out various landmarks as they headed out of the city. Mishka and Sacha were not paying any attention as they had likely heard it all before, so Rachel listened to them instead. Her friend had been to Lisbon on numerous occasions, but never to Fátima, so Sarah was clearly concentrating on the commentary.

At first, the men in front spoke in English about how much some crew members, whose names Rachel didn't recognise, had drunk the night before. Once they tired of that conversation, they moved on to the subject of work and Rachel's ears pricked up as she leaned forwards, pretending to look out of the window. She was disappointed as they almost immediately switched to Russian and their tone became more serious. The only thing she could make out was the Russian word for death and the name of Sosa. Gutted she hadn't continued her study of Russian, she resigned herself to sitting back in her seat with a sigh.

Sarah raised her eyebrows. "Serves you right," she said happily.

Rachel drifted in and out of sleep on the journey until she heard the guide relating the story of the three shepherd children who had seen a vision of the Virgin Mary on multiple occasions over several days in 1917. The apparitions had been approved by the Vatican and the site had become a Catholic pilgrimage since then. They would see a modern Basilica called Our Lady of Fátima and the Chapel of Apparitions. It wasn't a site where miracles had occurred as some sites were, but one that held spiritual significance for Roman Catholics.

Rachel was interested in history as her degree had been in the subject so she paid attention to the story. The guide ended her talk by telling them that two of the children had died during the influenza pandemic following the First World War and that the third had become a nun.

"Fascinating," said Sarah once the guide stopped talking. "I read a few books about flu pandemics recently – I love medical history. We're always living in fear of the next one."

Rachel nodded. "Swine flu didn't turn out to be the pandemic, did it?"

"No it didn't, but one mutation will be all it takes and

huge swathes of the world's population could be taken out in a matter of months, or even weeks due to modern travel."

"I'm pleased to hear you two having such a positive conversation," Gilbert Bradshaw's voice cut in.

"Sorry, Dad. I can't help it. That WWI pandemic was awful, you know. It killed more people than the war, some estimates suggest over 50 million people worldwide. At the time, people were so pleased the so-called war to end all wars was over, it didn't get as much coverage as it would have if the Government hadn't been so keen to raise morale. Nurses and doctors were the heroes, putting themselves in harm's way, caring for the sick. Many of them died."

"I think that's quite enough of that subject, Sarah, please. Your father and I would like to enjoy a spiritually uplifting visit, not a health lecture, if you don't mind."

"Sorreeey!"

"It was a bit depressing, but you can tell me more about it another time. Better still, recommend the book."

Sarah smiled. "You're right. Sorry, Mum."

The coach drew to a halt and passengers started to alight. Rachel was nudging Sarah to move so that she could be close to the restaurant staff, but her friend decided to be obtuse and wouldn't budge.

"If I have to stop talking medicine, you can certainly stop chasing murderers," she whispered.

"What are you whispering about?"

"I was just saying to Rachel how good it was she could forget about work for a while." The girls' guffaws drew a look of consternation from Mary, while Gilbert merely shrugged his shoulders.

"They're happy, Mary. Come on, let's get you into that Basilica before it starts to rain."


Rachel and Sarah managed to get away from the crowds of pilgrims to grab a hot coffee from a café. As luck would have it, Mishka and Sacha joined them.

"Are you enjoying day out, Nurse?" Sacha asked.

"Please call me Sarah. I'm out of uniform, so forget about the nurse bit for today."

"Okay, Sarah."

"This is my friend, Rachel. You've seen her dining with me and my parents."

"Delighted, Rachel. We have met, but not properly. I am Sacha and this is Mishka." Sacha seemed pleased to talk, and if Rachel had to tolerate a small degree of flirtation, she decided it was all in a good cause.

"Do join us. Are you enjoying the visit?"

"I would enjoy it more if it were not so cold, but we are Catholic so a good place to pay our respects to Our Lady. The shrine was beautiful." Mishka's eyes watered as he recounted his experience. "Sacha thinks I'm foolish, but I felt Her presence."

"Enough of that, man. Can't you just keep these things to yourself? No-one likes to talk religion. I'm sure Sarah and Rachel would rather enjoy sensible conversation."

"We are in a spiritual place, so it's okay. I'm pleased you had an experience, Mishka," said Sarah, always one to defend the underdog, tapping his arm.

"What about you, Rachel? How are you enjoying your cruise?" Sacha chose to move away from the topic his friend had started and they ended up having two conversations, Sarah with Mishka and Rachel with Sacha.

"I'm enjoying it so far. Such a shame about your boss, though. I was only speaking to him on the way down to Southampton. It makes one think, doesn't it?"

Sacha looked disappointed that his charm wasn't having the desired effect and frowned. "Death is always sad, but in the case of our boss – I hope you don't mind me saying, but he was a bad man. You will find it hard to discover anyone who is sorry about his passing."

"He must have had some good points."

Sacha's scowl answered the question for her. "I fear not. Mish couldn't stand him, he was always giving him trouble. Pash – he is now boss – also hated him. Sosa bullied people, men and women, but I hear he was extra cruel to women, so be pleased you didn't know him well."

Sarah and Mishka had stopped talking, and Mishka looked angry.

"The world is better place without that man. He caused trouble wherever he went. It's good he died. I was often tempted to feed him nuts. We all knew about his allergy."

Mishka roared with laughter. Sarah was astonished.

"One minute, you're telling me about your religious experience, and in the next breath you are joking about the death of another human being."

Mishka looked devastated. "I apologise. I should not have been disrespectful, but that man did not deserve to live. I would never have done what I said; it was joke in poor taste."

They finished up their drinks, and as Mary and Gilbert joined them, the two men excused themselves. The Bradshaws and Rachel were happy to get back on the coach having enjoyed the visit, but everywhere had been just a little too cold. Rachel and Sarah had been scolded by Mary for not bringing warm coats; Rachel acknowledged their error, but Sarah saw it as nagging and reacted accordingly. Peace had been restored only when Mary told Sarah how much she liked Jason.

The journey back to the ship was pleasant. Rachel felt rejuvenated, having caught up on her sleep and been out in the bracing cold wind. Mary and Gilbert appeared to have enjoyed the visit with Mary remarking on how peaceful it had been inside the chapel, despite the crowds.

"People were so respectful. It was atmospheric."

Rachel pondered Mishka's confessions and wondered

if he had needed the religious experience in order to assuage his guilt, if he was the person who'd managed to tamper with the bread his late boss had eaten. It seemed odd that he would confess to thoughts of wanting to murder his boss, but she reasoned that he must feel safe because the death was an assumed accident, so he could enjoy the role play, even down to his pretend confession. Some murderers enjoyed the 'catch me if you can' bravado following a killing. Could Mishka be the one they were looking for?

She was determined to find out.

# Chapter 13

After four days without any real exercise, Rachel felt dreadful. The additional lack of sleep wasn't helping, she reminded herself while looking at her mobile to check the time: 5.30am. Thoughts had been whirring around her brain all night; she hadn't managed to see Jason the night before as Sarah had insisted they take her parents to the officers' dining room again as promised.

Although annoyed at having to take her eye off the case, Rachel had found the evening refreshing. The respite turned out to be a welcome break for all of them – the whole of the medical team had been there and Jason managed to join them, much to the delight of the Bradshaws. Mary Bradshaw was gushing over Jason, and both she and Gilbert were impressed at being introduced to Captain Jenson who welcomed them aboard and sang Sarah's praises. What more could they have asked for? The evening had been topped off with a late show and they all retired to bed exhausted, apart from Jason who had been called away shortly after dinner.

As a result of the pleasant evening, though, Rachel had forgotten to tell anyone about the information she had found in Sosa's notes and possible motives arising from them, or about the McCauleys. It appeared from financial entries that Sosa may had gathered dirt on all his colleagues and was blackmailing each one independently. It wasn't clear whether they knew about each other, but it did give a number of people motive to kill him. What she didn't know was what he'd had on each of them and whether it would be enough to cause them to resort to murder.

She hauled herself out of bed, realising sleep wouldn't be returning anytime soon, and donned her tracksuit. A run would help clear her head. At home she ran at least once a day, sometimes twice, and usually when on board the *Coral,* she would run and go to the gym most mornings. It was the perfect time to get some fitness in while most people were still in bed.

With renewed vigour, she made her way up to deck sixteen. It was still dark, but the running track was well lit. After stretching for ten minutes, she pulled up a playlist on her iPhone, put her earphones in to listen to music and started to run.

She had done ten laps without coming across anyone, but now she passed by a crewman jogging in the opposite direction.

"Morning, ma'am."

She noticed a gapped smile where two top teeth were missing. "Morning," she replied before turning her head back to face the direction she was running in, too late to avoid a foot sticking out and it sent her sprawling across the deck. The dew in the air meant her hands and body slid on the running track, and as she landed and put her left hand down to save her body from too much damage, she felt sharp pain in her right hip and a kick to the back of her ribs. Her assailant then left her to groan and she rolled over on to her back to try to assess the damage.

The crewman who had been running laps stopped when he found her on the ground, staring at a grazed hand and side. Her mobile phone had landed a few yards away, yanking the earphones from her ears. Her right ear felt sore from the force.

"Ma'am, are you okay?"

"Just a fall, I think I must have tripped over something." Rachel wasn't sure whether this crewman had deliberately distracted her prior to the attack and she was on her guard in case he was going to finish the job. She wasn't going to give him the satisfaction of feeling he had been successful if either was the case.

"You're bleeding, I'm going to call for medics. Please stay here."

Rachel put a hand to her right hip where he pointed and saw a deep cut. It was at that moment she realised she had been stabbed at the same time as kicked.

She felt light-headed by the time the man returned. He had managed to find a towel and pressed it firmly against her hip while reassuring her help was on the way.

"What's your name?"

"Sean," he answered. "You're Rachel, aren't you?"

"How do you know?"

"I'm the security team steward, I've seen you with the chief sometimes. He likes you." The gap-toothed smile was broad. "Someone attacked you – I saw them run away just as I turned the bend down the other end of the deck."

"Did you see who it was?"

"No, sorry, I was too far away and they were wearing dark clothing. Even with the lights, I just saw a dark shadow running in the opposite direction."

At that moment, Sarah and Alex Romano, the junior doctor, appeared. "Rachel, what happened? I don't believe this." Sarah's worried shaking of the head and angry tone were filled with pent up frustration.

Rachel grimaced. "I don't know really. Someone tripped me up, then attacked me from behind."

Alex applied further pressure on top of the blood-soaked towel while Sarah handed him a pressure bandage from her bag. Security Officer Ravanos arrived – at least he and Rachel had met before. Ravanos spoke in quiet tones with Sean while Sarah and the doctor helped Rachel up.

"Will you be able to walk if we help you?" Sarah asked, calmer now, and Rachel was pleased she had returned to competent nurse rather than neurotic friend mode. Rachel nodded and gritted her teeth as the pain shot through her hip when she stood up. Her head felt fuzzy, but she knew that as soon as they got her to the medical centre, she would be able to lie down and have a drink. Sarah shook her head constantly, as if by doing so she would be better able to understand what had happened to her friend.

"I'm afraid we're going to need to stitch that wound, I think it's too deep to glue," said Alex. If he had any thoughts of déjà vu, he was keeping them to himself, for which Rachel was grateful. There would be enough ribbing once the concern died down later, she was certain of that. The infirmary on deck two was a place that was all too familiar to her from previous cruises, and not somewhere she enjoyed being in the capacity of patient.

Dr Bentley had been called; Alex Romano knew the chief medical officer would want to oversee treatment of his favourite and most dreaded passenger. The concerned look said it all as he arrived just after Rachel had been assisted on to a couch.

"Rachel Prince, you have to be the most accident-prone passenger ever to board this ship."

"If only they were accidents," she replied sheepishly.

"Indeed. I've had to dismiss Chief Waverley to wait in Gwen's office, otherwise he'd be having apoplexy with worry. I've called Gwen to calm him down while we see to you. Are you up to date with tetanus?"

"Yes, just a couple of months ago."

"Right. Sarah, we'll need some immunoglobulin."

"Already drawn up, I was just about to give it." She

looked at Rachel. "Sorry, this one will hurt."

Rachel turned towards her left side slightly to allow the injection to be given in the buttock.

"Ouch! You weren't kidding, were you?"

"I don't suppose it will teach you to stay out of trouble?"

"Excuse me, but up until now, you were alright with me helping Jason."

"That's before I realised you could be in danger."

"Ladies, could we keep this for later? Sarah, can I take a look at the wound, please?"

Rachel felt increasingly weak, but she couldn't resist checking the damage herself as the pressure dressing was removed. There was a two-inch gash to her right hip.

"Ooh, that doesn't look nice." She took a gulp of water from a glass Sarah had handed her. Her friend was being much more sympathetic after seeing the wound.

Dr Bentley irrigated the gash in her hip with disinfectant and stitched the knife wound after using local anaesthetic to numb the area.

"It's not too deep, you'll be glad to know. Four stitches and I'll give you a course of antibiotics to take. I take it you're not allergic to penicillin?"

"No."

"Good. I'll leave Sarah to tend your other wounds before our CSO forces his way in here."

Dr Bentley left the infirmary shaking his head.

Sarah's eyebrows were doing their familiar upside-down V thing when Rachel pulled her eyes away from the dressing on her hip.

"What? How was I to know someone would object so strongly to my involvement?"

Sarah cleaned Rachel's grazed left hand and thigh. "You're right. It's not you I'm angry with; I'm more annoyed with myself for even thinking it was a good idea to let you do this. Not to mention Jason and Waverley, they should have known better."

"Speak of the devil." Rachel saw the security chief coming in through the double doors, followed by Raggie, the medical team steward. Raggie was carrying a tray of coffee.

"I know you like strong coffee, Miss Rachel, so I brought it up myself. Can I get you something to eat?"

"Actually, that would be great. I feel ravenous for some reason – it must be all that lost blood."

"Full English coming up, then."

"Er hum," Waverley coughed. "I can't apologise enough, Rachel. If I had suspected for one moment you might be in any danger, I would never have asked you to involve yourself in this business. I've been selfish and that was wrong of me."

"Don't worry about it, I don't think I was in any real danger. I think this was more of a warning to stop asking questions. They had time to do a lot more damage with the knife if they had wanted to."

"And perhaps we should take that warning seriously,"

said Sarah.

"Quite," said Waverley. "I don't suppose you can tell me any more about the incident? Sean has filled me in on what he saw, which wasn't very much, to be honest."

"Me neither. I was running laps when someone tripped me up. I thought I had a vision of a fox when I was on the ground, then whoever it was added a few warning blows. I was kicked and stabbed, but not anywhere that would cause serious damage. Either the attacker didn't know what they were doing or it was, as I've said, a warning. I'm inclined to think it was the latter."

"I agree, it certainly looks that way. It must have been someone who knows about you, though, which should narrow it down."

"I've quizzed the waiters in the Club Restaurant, that's all, but you forget, I ate openly with Sarah, Jason and her parents on day one, and we met in Creams yesterday. If someone was observing what the investigation was uncovering, they may have guessed I was involved."

"In which case, anyone could have attacked you, but I'm leaning towards one of the restaurant staff. I think our killer is among that group and it's a small list."

"Possibly, but there's still Brenda's father and—"

Waverley looked as though he'd been hit. "Brenda's father? And who else?"

Rachel realised Jason hadn't got around to informing his boss of other suspects being present on the ship and she'd let it out.

"Sorry, Jason found out on the first sea day. He was tired and must have forgotten to mention it; I don't think he would be hiding it from you."

Waverley huffed loudly and his frown caused her to feel sorry for Jason, but how was she to know Jason hadn't told his boss already?

She changed the subject. "Is there CCTV footage of the running deck?"

"Yes, there is. Ravanos and Mitchell are going through it now. I'll let you know if we find anything."

Rachel poured a second mug of coffee as Raggie arrived with breakfast. "I brought you some too, Nurse. I know you've been on call all night."

"Thank you, Raggie. I don't know where we would all be without you."

"I'll leave you to it, then," announced Waverley sullenly. He jumped up from the end of Rachel's bed and stomped out of the infirmary.

"I'm so sorry," said Rachel to Sarah as she buttered a slice of toast and tucked into a sausage. "I didn't know Jason hadn't told him."

"Me neither. He'll have his reasons, but I wouldn't like to be in his shoes right now." Sarah's colour was coming back; Rachel realised her friend worried about her and she'd probably had little sleep.

"How was your night?"

"Full of accident-prone drunken revellers, since you

ask."

"Well, it is Christmas."

"Not yet it isn't, but the party's started early for some. Anyway it was nothing too dramatic, just lots of call outs. Alex was on too so he helped out."

Alex was a popular member of the medical team, and according to Sarah, he never ducked out of his duties – unlike some doctors her friend said she'd worked with on land.

"I assume the revellers were passengers." Rachel enjoyed hearing about Sarah's work and the antics people got up to when on board. If she didn't know Sarah, she would think every cruise was a dream and no-one ever got sick or injured, but it was hard for her to imagine a cruise like that anymore.

"Passengers mostly. A couple of teenagers play-acting ended up in the pool and one of them cut his foot after he dropped a bottle on his way in."

"Is he alright?"

"In terms of injury, yes – a small amount of glue required. But he won't be alright if the head pool attendant finds him because the pool had to be drained, scrubbed, disinfected and refilled."

"Blimey! I didn't even know the pools were uncovered at this time of year."

"That's the other thing that annoyed the pool attendants. They are in daylight hours, but not at night. The lads thought it would be fun to go for a starlight swim; the idiots removed the cover, and then got the shock of their lives when security gave them an ear-bashing before escorting them back to their rooms. They got their comeuppance, though, as Ravanos knocked up all the parents to tell them about the incident and warn them that if their offspring didn't behave responsibly from now on, they would be escorted off ship in Madeira and would have to make their own way home."

Rachel laughed. "I'm sure that did the trick."

"I think it did. Then I got called to see a woman who was vomiting."

"Not the dreaded norovirus?"

"No, too much alcohol. By the time I arrived, she was fast asleep and her partner apologised for calling me out."

Rachel and Sarah chatted for ages about Sarah's night before she checked the clock. "I'd better go and shower before morning surgery. You can leave whenever you want to. Do you want Raggie to get you some clean clothes?"

"No thanks, I'll put on a pair of your scrubs and take a shower when I get back to my room." Rachel rose timidly from the bed. "And Sarah?"

"What?"

"Not a word about this to your parents."

"I wouldn't dare. They still don't know we've had a death on board. Mum would go ballistic."

"She would, poor Mary. On that topic, you need to give her a bit more latitude. You know she means well."

"I have been a bit sharp with her. I don't know why, except that the more she pushes me and Jason together, the more I want to rebel."

"None of us likes to be told what to do by our parents, Sarah, but she's on holiday in your domain. She's struggling to maintain an element of control. When you're home, it's her territory, but here, well—"

"You are right, of course. I bet you don't have these issues with your mum."

"Not really, but I'm engaged so it's different. Also Mum and Dad have David and Amy plus a whole congregation relying on them to keep them in one piece, whereas you're all your parents have."

"Now I feel terrible. Jason said the same thing last night, but I snapped at him."

"Why?"

"I told him that someone who doesn't even see his parents is in no position to lecture me on how to behave towards mine."

"Ouch! I hope you retracted some of that."

"Not really, but he doesn't take offence. I love that about him; he just told me that my reaction showed he was right."

Rachel laughed. "He really gets you, doesn't he?"

Sarah smiled, gooey eyed.

"Anyway, speaking of loved ones, I need to go and FaceTime Carlos before we are too far away from land. I still have a signal."

# Chapter 14

After showering carefully to avoid too many splashes over the stitched wound, Rachel felt refreshed, although she could have done without the ache to her ribs and sharp pains in the right hip as the anaesthetic wore off. She looked in the mirror and had a conversation with herself about staying away from dangerous situations, but she really couldn't blame herself as she just hadn't anticipated this one. There was no doubt in her mind that it had been a warning rather than an intention to do her more serious harm. Nevertheless, the attack demonstrated that the perpetrator was willing to go to extreme measures to prevent discovery.

It was high time she found out what was going on. One thing was now clear, though, and that was that Sosa had definitely been murdered, but by whom was still a puzzle. The list of suspects with motive had grown rather than reduced.

Rachel sat at the mirrored desk in her room and wrote notes about everyone she had so far spoken to, along with alibis and motives. Motive in a way was fairly straightforward – the dead man had been a nasty piece of work who'd used violence, threat and extortion to get his way and had more than one target. The most likely killer would be someone who either worked with him closely or had been threatened by him in some way. Brenda's father and Sosa's sister being on board the ship complicated matters. Although his sister was unlikely to have a motive at this stage, Rachel put a question mark over her name, and that of the brother-in-law.

While showering, she had cast her mind back to boarding day and was almost positive that the man she had witnessed Sosa arguing with when he'd alighted from the coach would turn out to be Brenda's father, although it could also have been his own brother-in-law. Rachel would ask Jason to pull up their identity photos, then she would know for certain. An argument in itself proved nothing, but it did add at least one passenger to the suspect list.

A knock at the door interrupted Rachel's ruminations. It couldn't be Sarah as she was still in surgery. She walked sheepishly over to the door and used the spy hole to see who was there. Satisfied it was friend rather than foe, she opened the door.

"Chief, we can't keep meeting like this," she quipped.

"May I come in?"

"Yes of course, but I'm not sure I can add anything to what I've already told you."

Waverley followed her inside and took a seat, glancing over at her notes still piled on the desk. She sat next to him.

"I see you're still keeping up with the case in spite of, er hum, what happened."

"I actually have a vested interest in finding out who killed your Mr Sosa now since someone clearly tried to warn me off. I don't like being attacked."

"Perhaps it's a warning you should heed for once." He smiled sullenly.

"Not a chance, and you wouldn't ask me to if you had the pain in your ribs that I have, not to mention the stab wound. I don't suppose CCTV told you who attacked me?"

"I'm afraid not, the person wore a hood and knew exactly where the cameras were, adding to the likelihood it was a crew member. As you're not going to back down, we should compare notes. I'm back in charge of the case."

"Really? That is good news, but how did that happen?"

"Brenda's in the clear – well as much as she can be, anyway. The coroner called an hour ago; it appears it was not an allergen at all and the toxic substance was in the whisky, not in the bread."

"Not an allergen? I thought Dr Bentley and the coroner were convinced it was anaphylaxis. Thank goodness for that, though – about Brenda, I mean." Rachel was genuinely pleased to hear some good news at last.

"And that's what it looked like. The coroner finally got round to doing a post-mortem this morning and found the man's gut had almost exploded. Apparently it's called caustic ingestion and has been confused with anaphylaxis in children who tend to drink harmful substances on occasion. It was the result of a detergent added to the whisky. The man had a liking for the stuff, and for some unknown reason didn't detect a change in taste. It's highly likely he himself thought it was an anaphylactic reaction from the bread he'd ingested at the same time, which is why he tried to reach for the epi-pens."

"That is a new one on me, has Dr Bentley been told?"

"Not yet, I'll tease him about it later. It's not often I get one over on him. It is good news as far as I'm concerned, but it does mean that we're back to square one – absolutely anyone could have spiked his drink. Needless to say, I've told the coroner what I think of his lackadaisical attitude."

"Was the bottle tested?"

"Yes and it was clear, but there was a minute residue in the bottom of the glass. Thanks to Goodridge, the glass was tested. The killer obviously switched the whisky bottles after death, but didn't have the opportunity to do the same with the empty glass. Goodridge told me you thought the pens had been removed and put back. I agree with your hypothesis and my theory is that the killer returned to the room to take the deadly whisky bottle and put the epi-pens back, and either forgot to switch the glass or was disturbed and had to leave."

"So the killer could have been in the room when the galley maid found the body?"

"Precisely – unless it was her, of course – and then they made haste before they were discovered while the maid called for help."

"Why do you think they removed the epinephrine if it wasn't anaphylaxis?"

"I wondered that myself and asked the coroner if an epi-pen could have helped, and he said it had been shown to slow down the reaction, so this tells us the killer had done their homework."

"Do you think it was one of the restaurant staff?"

"I do. It can't have been Brenda's father because he would have had no access to Sosa's room. He wouldn't even know where to look."

"Unless, of course, someone told him."

"You're not suggesting Brenda, I hope. She didn't even know her father was on board until Goodridge told her the other night – something she kept from me until I spoke to her after I'd seen you in the infirmary. I've also had words with Goodridge about the matter."

Rachel wasn't quite as certain as Waverley seemed to be about ruling out Brenda's father so soon, but she decided not to burst his bubble. He had only just been reinstated as head of the investigation; it would be best not to poke the bear or he'd warn her off like he usually did.

"I'm not certain you should continue with your involvement, though, Rachel. It could get dangerous."

"As I said, that's not going to happen, chief. I either work with you or behind your back, and I'm sure you wouldn't want me to do that, especially as I might come to harm."

Waverley heaved a sigh, the resignation apparent on his face. "Alright, but be careful and keep me in the loop. We're leaving it for appearances' sake that it was a probable error from the catering side and that Brenda is still the person responsible for the mistake. We'll let the restaurant staff continue believing that I'm off the case for now. It will keep the killer feeling secure, thinking they are safe, and that's what I want them to believe."

"Good plan and one that makes sense. So I'll continue to liaise with Jason as if he's in charge in case the killer is watching."

"Precisely. When they are lulled into a false sense of security, they will slip up and we'll be ready for them. I'm as keen as you are to find whoever is responsible as they tried to implicate my wife."

"By chance rather than design, I think, chief. They wouldn't have known Sosa was going to order room service, but they obviously knew he would take a drink before work."

"Implying?"

"That the perpetrator knew his habits."

"You're right and that is building a stronger case for

our murderer to be a member of the crew. It will be one of the restaurant staff, we just need to find out which one. Anyway, I'm pleased to see you're looking better. Be careful and try to let someone know where you are at all times. I don't want you disappearing on me."

"Aye, aye, chief."

Waverley let himself out with the bounce returned to his step. Rachel smiled after him, feeling guilt pangs that she hadn't mentioned Sosa's sister and brother-in-law or the argument she'd witnessed when leaving the bus on embarkation day. If Jason hadn't told the chief about Sosa's family, he probably had a reason not to, and she herself wanted to look at photo ID before letting anyone know about the argument.

She went back to the desk and looked at her notes, bearing in mind that the cause of death was now totally different to what they had imagined, and therefore the timeline had just lengthened from an opportunistic few minutes to around eight hours. It was likely that Sosa would have drunk whisky on the night before his trip to London, so the bottle had most likely been spiked during the time he was off the ship on embarkation day.

Another knock at the door had her wondering whether she was really on a cruise ship at all. This time it was Jason. He was as happy as Waverley had been.

"I heard about the attack, Rachel. I'm sorry, I bet Sarah's going to give me a hard time over it later."

"Of that I have no doubt, but it wasn't your fault. It

just means that we have been looking in the right place so far."

"Have you heard the news?"

"Yes, you've not long missed Waverley. He came to tell me to stay off the case, but we agreed I would keep looking, especially as he doesn't want anyone else to know the real cause of death has been discovered."

"I thought it would be good to compare notes in private rather than in a public place, is that alright?"

"Of course, take a seat and I'll get us some coffee."

Once they were settled, Rachel placed Sosa's notes and photos on to the table so that Jason could take a look through, and she handed him her own notes of the case so far. Rachel sipped coffee while Jason read through the pile she had marked as relevant.

"So he's had a private detective following his wife and son, with pictures of their whereabouts and dates. What I don't understand is why the sudden interest? These only date back four months and the letters stopped being delivered a few years ago."

"I had the same thought, and then I looked through some more documents. Look." She handed him a copy of the letter that had rekindled Sosa's interest. "This letter came from his father's solicitor. It appears that Mr Sosa Snr wasn't that fond of our Stefan either. The majority of his estate has been left to his only grandson, with a small sum of 1,200 Cuban Pesos – the equivalent of around £1,000 – to Sosa and 6,500 Pesos – around £5,000 – to his sister. If anything happens to Michael (Mikey) Jones, then the estate would revert back as an equal split between Stefan Sosa and Stella Gonzalez. The letter is dated a month before Sosa hired a private investigator to find his wife and son.

"Their new names and location were found a fortnight ago while Sosa was on the previous cruise, so he obviously went to London when the ship reached Southampton to track down his wife, probably assuming his son would be home for the Christmas break. I don't think for one minute he would have mentioned to her that his son was the likely heir to a small fortune."

"I see," said Jason, continuing to peruse the letter in his hand. He then turned to a copy of the will that accompanied the document and whistled. "Wow! His father was wealthy – by your calculation, the estate is worth £1million."

Rachel nodded. "So that gives the sister and brother-in-law ample motive to track down his son also."

"What if the solicitor in Cuba has done the same and found Mikey? Perhaps he and his mother do know," said Jason. "And what do you think Sosa had in store for his son?"

"I've been thinking about that too. If Christine was aware of Mikey's fortune and shared the news with her family, and if she suspected her son was in danger, there is also motive for her to want to get rid of Sosa – not to mention his violent record with them. As for what Sosa was going to say or do to his son, we'll never know. It is a possibility, albeit a remote one, that he was going to come clean and make amends for his past."

"If the man had changed in any way I would agree with you, Rachel, but that's not the picture we're getting."

"In which case, his son would have been in mortal danger, and that alone might account for Brenda's father being on board. I had forgotten until earlier that I'd witnessed Sosa arguing with a passenger on the dockside on embarkation day. That has to be either the ex-father-in-law or Paulo Gonzalez. I'm certain the man was British, so I think it likely it was the former."

Jason took in a deep breath. "There is real motive here, but if it was Richard Jones, Brenda's father, he would have needed help from an accomplice on board."

"And that brings us back to Brenda," Rachel finished.

Jason groaned. "Just when I thought it was all so simple. It could be that Stella and Paulo Gonzalez were in cahoots with Sosa and they were coming together for a planning meeting."

"Unless they were going to dissuade him from doing anything stupid, knowing the kind of man he was."

"Okay, we'll keep an open mind about them for the time being."

"Also, from the notes and pictures on the left, there is evidence Sosa was blackmailing at least four of his colleagues. I have found evidence of regular entries of money into Sosa's bank account from them." Rachel pointed to a financial ledger detailing the payments."

Jason frowned. "So we have Pash, Mishka, Danielle and Claudia Kitova all paying him off. That does give us another angle to work on. The only name missing is Sacha."

"Yes, so if blackmail was the motive, he's in the clear. Mishka actually admitted he would have been tempted to feed Sosa nuts, but I think he was joking. Anyway, he obviously believed nuts to be the cause of death, so that makes him an unlikely candidate too. Equally the man could have been killed by Richard Jones or by his own sister and the restaurant staff are just glad to be rid of him."

"Okay, so what do we know? We know he was blackmailing Danielle to do his bidding, and according to this – something she neglected to mention – he was also extorting money from her. So we urgently need to find out what he had on the others. It does explain why they've all been so cagey and unhelpful. There have been rumours that Pash is having an affair with the casino manager's wife. It wouldn't be the first affair he's had so I think we can assume that's what he was under the cosh for, but I'll get confirmation. I'm concerned Claudia Kitova is on this list because she's the one I'd crossed off from the start as we didn't find any links between her and Sosa. What's more, I like her. One thing is certain, the opportunistic brute had a blackmail list."

"That's about the sum of it. So it seems that the

majority of people who crossed his path had motive to kill him. We just don't know what that was."

"I'm beginning to know how they feel," said Jason, scowling.

"Me too." Rachel laughed.

"Top priority, we need to find out what Sosa had on Mishka and Claudia and confirm that Pash's affair was what he was being blackmailed about. I'll come down heavy on them."

"That would tell them we suspect murder. Why don't we do it a different way? Remember, we have a secret weapon – Bernard."

After she'd explained her plan, Jason left to update Waverley on the latest findings. Rachel agreed to meet them with Sarah in Waverley's office at 2pm so that they would all be in the picture.

# Chapter 15

The Bradshaws and Sarah were already seated in the Club Restaurant when Rachel arrived for lunch. She tried hard not to limp, but her right hip was sore and the stitches pulled with every step. The eagle-eyed Mary Bradshaw didn't miss the signs, as her concerned look showed. Hoping Sarah had made up a cover story, Rachel would wait until the Bradshaws brought it up.

Pash marched ahead of her at speed, pretending not to notice the limp, but she was certain he had seen it when she went to the desk – if he hadn't been the cause of it in the first place. He was the most ambitious among the waiters and high up on her suspect list, not to mention the fact she found him hard to like.

"Trust your instinct," her father had always told her as she was growing up. "It will keep you out of many a tricky situation." The advice had become a major part of who she was and often helped her solve crimes, both on and off cruise ships, but it would never be as reliable as good, solid evidence.

"Hello, Rachel. Sarah told us about your accident this morning. I hope you haven't done yourself too much damage?" Mary Bradshaw clasped her hand as Rachel gingerly sat down.

"No, just a few grazes, that's all. I'm fine."

Gilbert Bradshaw winked. "You should stay away from slippery running tracks early in the morning. Sarah says you were fiddling with your earphones when you slipped. There's a lot of moisture in the air at this time of year."

"Anyway, Mum, Dad," said Sarah, "I'm starving. What are we going to eat?"

At that moment, Mishka arrived to take their order. Having escaped any further enquiries about her 'fall', Rachel relaxed and enjoyed lunch while keeping one eye on how the waiters were behaving. Pash was attentive to the Bradshaws, but almost rude to Rachel, and he was definitely avoiding eye contact. Mary asked him about his home and Rachel was surprised to hear that he had a wife and four children whom he supported by sending money home each month.

"It must get lonely without your family, especially as they're so young."

*I think he more than compensates with the casino manager's wife*, thought Rachel, trying hard not to express her distaste when he answered.

"I miss them every day, ma'am. The children are so good and my wife is beautiful. Never a day goes by when I don't think of them, but we are poor in India and the money I earn here is much better than I would get at home."

"Poor man," said Mary after he'd left. "I don't know how he copes, being away from his children. We miss you, Sarah, and you're an adult; it must be impossible to be without his wife and children."

"I'm sure he manages." Rachel heard herself reacting in a way she wouldn't normally do; perhaps it was due to the pain in her hip, but it didn't escape Sarah's notice. Rachel saw her friend raise her eyebrows and give her a warning look. Fortunately, Mary Bradshaw had moved on to explaining how she and Gilbert had missed Sarah when she went to university and then joined Queen Cruises, but how they were so happy that she had now met Jason.

"All things work together for good," her husband said, quoting a snippet of a Bible verse from the book of Romans.

Sarah had been looking uncomfortable, but she visibly relaxed as soon as Jason was mentioned. *She's got it bad*, thought Rachel. Apart from the issues that her friend's beau had from being stationed in Afghanistan, and his trust problems from a broken engagement, he was a perfect choice. Rachel shook the thoughts away as she didn't want to be reminded of her own trust issues.

After dinner, they parted ways as the Bradshaws said they were going to the art gallery on board to browse before attending an art auction, then Mary was going to the hairdresser's. They were enjoying exploring the ship and engaging in as many activities as they could.

Rachel patted Sarah's arm. "Thanks for giving me a cover story; it was as close to the truth as it could have been, so we don't have to feel too guilty."

Sarah put her arm through Rachel's. "How are you feeling, really? And what was that all about over dinner with Pash?"

"I'll tell you on the way downstairs. Come on, we're meeting Jason and Waverley, who's now back on the case."

"I did hear that, he came to see Graham and told him about the new cause of death. He enjoyed lecturing him on caustic ingestion and Graham let him wax lyrical for a while, then told him about a recent paper he'd read on the topic in relation to paediatrics in America. Graham went into the research paper in great detail until Waverley's eyes glazed over, then the friendly one-upmanship came to an end and they went to eat in the officers' dining room."

Rachel laughed as she imagined the two chiefs sparring with each other over Dr Bentley's rare and understandable mistaken diagnosis of the dead man. She updated Sarah on what she and Jason had discussed this morning and where they were with the investigation.

"This is a difficult one for me, Rachel, because I feel that man deserved to die and I hate feeling this way. It's not right that anyone should be murdered, no matter how horrible they are."

Rachel understood the emotions her friend was going through; she went through them regularly in her police work. Some people were such terrible human beings it was hard at times to remain objective, but it wasn't her job to judge. That was down to the courts. She had to keep the peace and investigate crime; that was her role, and for the most part she loved her work.

Waverley and Jason were seated in the comfortable chairs in the chief's office when they arrived. Waverley invited them in with a wave of his hand before getting up and closing the blinds enough to allow light in while restricting anyone else's view of who was in the room.

"Drinks, ladies?" Waverley was remaining chipper and Rachel wondered if Jason had filled him in on the will situation yet, or on the Gonzalez's presence. They both requested coffee and sat on the sofa opposite to Jason and the chief.

"Jason has filled me in on the findings from the contents of Sosa's safe. I must say the man was most unpleasant and the information has muddied the waters somewhat. It's going to be very difficult to find out who spiked the whisky, but we might be able to eliminate a few of the suspects if we can pull together any verifiable alibis for the timeframe and find out what people are hiding. The most obvious person was staring us in the face all the time."

Rachel gawped. "You can't mean Claudia Kitova?"

"Why ever not? She had motive plus opportunity and

she was the last person to see Sosa alive. She would know where to get detergent from and would have easy access to his room."

"Surely any crew member would have access to detergent, if that's what was used?" said Sarah. "Most crew members would be able to sneak into a room if they really wanted to; they would just need to distract a room steward for a moment and borrow a key card."

"We really must improve our security on board this vessel. I'm not having people believing they can just march into rooms without permission, and that includes you, Miss Prince." The cough and the redness travelling from Waverley's neck to his face told Rachel it was time to move the conversation on.

"What about the other suspects?" she asked.

"I've a good mind to arrest them all right now and throw them off at the next port, but we don't want to alert them just yet that we're on to any of them."

"We have uncovered one thing," said Jason. "Mishka Prostakov has been supplying the crew with cannabis – that's what he is hiding. He's been under surveillance for some time, but finally we have video evidence. Security recruited a new team member who joined the ship in Southampton. She's been working undercover as a junior waitress. It turns out that today has been our lucky day – she caught him out by pretending to buy some for herself and has it all on film. We're holding fire for now in case he's our murderer and Janet is continuing with her undercover work, getting to know all the waiters."

"Wow! That is useful."

"You see, Rachel, we don't just twiddle our thumbs," said Waverley pointedly.

"I never thought you did, but it's still a big leap to go from selling some cheap pot to murder. I don't think it's him."

"The payments have been increasing, though, so he may have got tired of the greedy Stefan Sosa," Jason countered.

Waverley sipped tea and nodded. "That's a good point, Goodridge. You certainly need to question him again and see what you can discover. I think it's time we shook things up and let them know we suspect murder."

Rachel wasn't convinced this was the best tactic, but conceded in her head that aggressive questioning could cause the killer to make a mistake.

"And then there's Pash and Danielle, not to mention the others," said Jason.

"What others?"

"The sister and brother-in-law, sir. I've just told the chief about them being on board, and about the will." Jason nodded to Rachel with a look that told her nothing remained hidden. "And, erm, your father-in-law, sir." Jason stuttered as he just about got the final few words out.

"Humph! There's no way Richard Jones is involved in this. I've spoken with him and he has assured me he knew nothing about Sosa being on board, and Brenda hadn't mentioned Sosa's behaviour to him in the past for fear of what he might do. He's on a surprise visit to pass on family Christmas presents and see his older daughter, that's all there is to it. No-one in the family had any knowledge of the will or Sosa's father's death and there the story ends. We're not wasting time chasing our tails while the killer is on board this ship, mocking us."

The decibels had risen along with the redness to Waverley's face. Jason shook his head at Rachel, warning her not to persist, but that was not going to happen.

"Chief, while I'm sure you're right, you cannot rule out a person with motive based on their word alone, otherwise we wouldn't be investigating any of them. People who kill do not generally put their hands up and own the crime until they are caught. That's our job."

Waverley's head snapped up from his drink. "This is not your investigation, Miss Prince. I can order you to stay out of it at a moment's notice, so watch your step!"

Sarah intervened. "It's been a stressful time for the chief, Rachel, so we must recognise that. He wouldn't want any of us not to investigate thoroughly to – how do you lot say it? – eliminate people from our enquiries."

The reverse psychology worked. "Of course not. I wasn't saying we wouldn't check alibis, but we do need to focus on the chief suspects, and in my book the prime suspect is Ms Kitova, and the second, Miss Danielle Barcellos, the wine waitress. Both had the most to lose."

Rachel clamped her mouth shut, not convinced she would be able to stand much more of this. *If you rule out the potential loss of a grandson and a fortune*, went unspoken. She decided not to antagonise the chief any further when they had just reeled him back from apoplexy, thanks to Sarah's subtlety. Past experience told her Waverley could be inordinately stubborn, but would come to his senses when the evidence turned up, and she would find the evidence with or without him, no matter who was guilty.

"Right, I'll leave it to you. Goodridge, interview the suspects again. Perhaps, on second thoughts, we'll not show our hand just yet about it being murder. Tell them you're just finalising your report for health and safety or something. I'll speak to my father-in-law again to clarify his boarding time and movements on embarkation day. Rachel, you can befriend Stella and Paulo Gonzalez. I've asked Graham Bentley to pull them in and inform them of the tragic death of Sosa, so you can pretend you're a counsellor or something like that and talk to them afterwards with Sarah, if you like.

"That's all for now, then. We have a plan and hopefully we'll at least manage to eliminate a few of these people from our enquiries, as Sarah so eloquently put it. Now, I have a meeting with the captain. Lock the door when you leave, Goodridge."

The three of them stared at the door as it closed behind Waverley in disbelief. Jason was the first to speak.

"It's not been easy on him. First he thinks Brenda

might be involved, then there's the euphoria that she isn't, and then I walk in and tell him that his father-in-law might also have a motive. It's going to take him time to process it all."

"I guess you omitted to mention that Brenda might have assisted him," Rachel said dryly.

"It's called drip-feeding information, Rachel. We do it in medicine all the time," said Sarah. "Too much information all at once can have a devastating effect; it's best to go slowly. Waverley will come to his senses; he's a just man underneath it all."

"But we can all be blind when it comes to those closest to us," said Rachel.

"We have enough to go on, and for now we follow the chief's instructions," said Jason.

Rachel's memory kicked in. "Is there any CCTV footage from embarkation day?"

"No, it's wiped every twenty-four hours. There's no coverage in the staff corridor as the company doesn't like spying on its staff. That said, more cameras are being installed all the time, so there will come a day when very few areas are without it. The cameras aren't live-monitored when they are in place. We just pull footage up when needed."

"Do you think I can have a look at the IDs of Richard Jones and the Gonzalez couple?"

"Yes, of course." Jason rose from the chair and walked over to Waverley's desk, switching on the desktop computer. He signed himself in and tapped a few buttons, bringing up three photos on screen.

Rachel stood next to him and pointed. "That's the man I saw arguing with Sosa on boarding day." She and Jason gave a collective sigh.

The name below was that of Richard Jones.

# Chapter 16

"I can't believe you really want me to impersonate a counsellor, Sarah. It doesn't feel right. What if these people are not murderers or accomplices in blackmail and they do need proper counselling?"

"You just say 'go on' and encourage them to speak, that's what most counsellors seem to do," said Bernard, who was sitting with them in Gwen's office waiting for the Gonzalez couple to arrive.

Sarah nudged him. "That's a low comment, Bernard, even for you."

Bernard grinned and puffed his chest out as only he could. "It's true, they don't say a lot, just ask questions. You're good at asking questions, Rachel."

"I still don't like it. Asking questions as a police officer is one thing, this is quite different. I know nothing about counselling."

"You know even less about nursing so we can't pretend you're a nurse, can we?" Sarah interrupted. "Anyway, you've counselled me through some difficult times, and you are a vicar's daughter."

"Oh and that makes me a counsellor by default, does

it? And friendship is different because you have done the same for me on multiple occasions."

"You're overthinking it, Rachel," said Bernard. "Consider it undercover work."

"I'm surprised Dr Bentley has agreed to this anyway. You could do it in your professional capacity as a nurse, either one of you."

"I would be too soft and miss the signals," said Sarah.

"And I would be too impatient; I don't hold to all this navel-gazing baloney."

"Bernard, you drive me to distraction at times," Sarah scolded.

Rachel laughed. Bernard's humour always won her over. "Alright, I'll just say 'go on' and hope they do! Failing that, I'll go into police mode and quiz them as suspects, then you'll be sorry."

"I'm pleased to see you're all enjoying yourselves." Gwen came into the office alongside Dr Bentley.

"It's Bernard's fault," said Sarah, still giggling. "Don't ever send him for counselling, whatever you do."

Bernard rolled his eyes to the sky, looking innocently at his boss.

"Don't you give me the innocent look, Bernard. I've been sorely tempted to do just that on numerous occasions so watch yourself, mate. Anyway, I'm pleased you've made them laugh. Rachel, are you ready?"

"I suppose so. Are you coming too, Gwen?"

"I'll stay in with you initially. We've decided to use this

room while Graham gives them the news, and then we'll both depart and leave you to your, erm, counselling."

"Are you sure you're happy to do this, Rachel?" asked Dr Bentley.

"I'm glad someone cares what I think about this; I seem to have been bulldozed into it as a matter of fact. But you know me – I can't keep my nose out of any investigation, so I'm resigned. It will be a good way of meeting the couple without stalking them."

"In that case, let's get it over with. I do wish Chief Waverley wouldn't interfere with the running of the medical centre."

Sarah squeezed Rachel's hand and Bernard gave her a nod of encouragement, but couldn't resist a word or two – "Go on" – to which the three of them laughed, leaving Gwen and Dr Bentley staring in bemusement.

"Right, you two children, get out of my office. We need it."

Sarah and Bernard left and Gwen called in the couple, who'd arrived in the waiting room as the others were leaving.

"Do come in, Mr and Mrs Gonzalez." They entered the office. Dr Bentley and Rachel stood. "Please, take a seat."

The confused couple sat on the small sofa, while Gwen, the doctor and Rachel sat in the chairs.

"Before we start, can I get you coffee?" asked Gwen as Raggie entered with a tray of tea and coffee and placed it on the table. Paulo Gonzalez spoke first.

"A coffee would be appreciated, thank you. I must ask what this is all about." His sharp eyes, hidden beneath designer spectacles, were already taking in the three people in front of him. He was tall and distinguished in appearance, and aged sixty. The latter fact, Rachel knew from his passenger information records.

"Quite," said Dr Bentley while Gwen poured coffees all round.

Stella Gonzalez had her brother's nose, Rachel thought, but there the likeness ended. She was beautiful: long brown hair, almost as long as Rachel's own, and deep green eyes behind the longest lashes she had ever seen that weren't false. The woman was slim but not thin and immaculately groomed and dressed. Her hand shook slightly when she picked up her coffee.

"I'm Dr Bentley, the senior medical officer on board the *Coral Queen*, this is our senior nurse, Sister Sumner, and this is Rachel Prince, our onboard counsellor."

Four eyes shot towards Rachel. "And why would we need a counsellor, Dr Bentley?" Gonzalez asked, still holding Rachel's gaze.

Dr Bentley ignored Gonzalez and addressed his wife. "Mrs Gonzalez, I understand you have a brother on board this ship, Stefan Sosa?"

"Really? Is Stefan on board? We haven't spoken for a while, I didn't know."

A flicker of the eyelids and loss of eye contact told

Rachel the woman was not telling the truth. She was now pleased to be here and sat back, observing closely.

"You didn't know?"

"If that's all this is about, doctor, I think we can leave now. We don't want to meet Stefan, he has hurt his family in many ways. Come on, darling, let's go."

Before Paulo Gonzalez had the chance to move, Gwen interceded. "You should hear what Dr Bentley has to say before you go. Please." She appealed to Stella who remained seated, causing her husband to rejoin her.

"I'm afraid I have some bad news, Mrs Gonzalez. Your brother was found dead in his cabin on the evening we left Southampton."

Stella almost spilt her coffee as her hand increased its shaking. "Found dead?"

"I'm sorry to say, yes. His body was returned to Southampton for a post-mortem later that night."

"Drink, I suppose. He drank too much, that was his problem."

"Paulo, don't. He was still my brother."

"Drink did have something to do with it, Mr Gonzalez, but not in the way you imply. Someone added something to his drink that resulted in a fatal reaction."

Rachel watched both responses closely and couldn't tell if they were good actors or they really didn't know Stefan was aboard, or that he was dead. It seemed unlikely, and Gonzalez was reacting a little too calmly for her liking.

"You mean he was poisoned? I'm afraid, doctor, he did have a knack of upsetting people so it doesn't come as a big surprise. That sort of thing happens in Cuba all the time, but I didn't expect it to occur on a cruise ship."

"Why would anyone want to poison him?" asked Stella, ignoring her husband and pushing his hand away.

"We're not sure yet. Our security team is investigating and I expect one of the team will be wanting to speak with you later today or tomorrow. I really am sorry to be the bearer of bad news. This must come as a big shock."

"Do you know anyone who might have intended to harm your brother?"

Gonzalez swung his head back in Rachel's direction. "Of course not! We've already told you, we didn't keep in touch."

Stella gripped his arm, quietening him, and spoke softly. "We lost touch around sixteen months ago. Stefan came to visit us in Cuba. He drank too much and became uncontrollable – he had always drunk, but not like he did then. One night, the liquor caused his tongue to become too loose and he insulted me and my parents. Paulo told him to be quiet, but he wouldn't stop. He ranted and raved at us all. My mother was dying, but he didn't seem to care. My father got up to hit him, but he was a frail old man. Stefan pushed him and he fell.

"Paulo could not take any more. He intervened, punched Stefan and threw him out of the house, telling him never to return. Stefan called me the next day to apologise, but I was still angry with him. He told me to tell our mother he was sorry. I told him to go to hell." Tears now ran down Stella's cheeks, causing her mascara to run.

"So you see, we had no reason to see the man again. We were not friends." Paulo's anger spilled over to compensate for his wife's tears.

"And did you ever see him again?" Rachel asked gently.

"A week later my mother died. I sent him a letter to inform him, but told him it would be better if he stayed away from the funeral because our father would not want him there. He was back on board your ship by then anyway."

Paulo stared angrily at his wife. "You never told me you contacted him. I bet you didn't tell your father either."

Stella hid her eyes in a handkerchief her husband had supplied before looking at him. "I didn't tell you because I knew you would be angry, like you are now. I told Father a few weeks after the funeral. I told him Stefan was their only son and he deserved to know. He nodded and we never spoke of it again."

Rachel almost felt pity for the wayward Stefan, being ordered to stay away from his own mother's funeral, but if he'd really wanted to be there, surely he would have made the effort to be reconciled with the family he had hurt so much.

"Did he reply to your letter?" she asked.

"No, I didn't hear from him again. I wrote to him six months ago to let him know that Father had died, but he didn't reply to that letter either."

"You knew he was on this ship, didn't you?" Her husband's voice became accusing.

"So what if I did? I wanted to tell him in person about the pain he'd caused our father, and that Father had chosen to write both of us out of his will as a result."

Dr Bentley and Gwen exited without the couple noticing while Rachel poured another round of coffee. She let the quiet hang for a few minutes before breaking it.

"Go on," she said, forcing herself not to smile.

"I'm sorry, Paulo. I knew you would refuse if I told you. I needed to see my brother and tell him how much he'd cost us, and now your business is failing I don't know what we're going to do. I wanted to ask him to speak to his son and see if Mikey would be generous to us." Stella turned to Rachel. "I'm not in the habit of begging, but things are difficult in Cuba. Without money, we are nothing."

"How did you know about the business?"

"I'm not stupid, Paulo. You were becoming distant, snappy. At first I thought it was another woman, then I sneaked a look in your office and found the rejected loan applications."

Paulo softened, pulling his wife into his arms and

allowing her to cry on his shoulder. He looked at Rachel.

"Things have been difficult, but what this silly woman doesn't know," he stroked his wife's hair, "is that I have a buyer for the business – an investor who is happy to keep me on – and we will have enough money from the sale to be quite comfortable for as long as we live. I should have told you, Stella, but I thought you would prefer not to know."

Stella had ceased crying and lifted her head up. "I'm not one of those stupid Cuban women who doesn't have a clue what's going on. I'm my mother's daughter," she said proudly. "So this whole trip has been a waste of time."

"In terms of begging that wretched brother of yours for money, yes, but we still have Christmas to look forward to." Turning to Rachel again, Gonzalez continued, "Stefan would never have agreed anyway, he was only interested in himself. I'm not even sure he knew where his son lived, let alone stood a chance of asking the young man for money. Any money he could have squeezed out of the boy would have been spent on Stefan Sosa, no-one else. My wife has always believed her brother was redeemable, but he wasn't. I won't speak ill of the dead any further, but the man was rotten right through with no good qualities to save him."

Stella nodded. "I've been silly, but I am sorry my brother is dead. Whether or not he was a bad man, he was the only brother I had."

"I'm afraid your brother had discovered where his son was." Rachel didn't fill Stella in on the marriage violence, but told her, "He hired a private investigator who traced his ex-wife to London. He also had the address of the university where your nephew is studying in his belongings. I don't think any contact would have been encouraged from either party, though."

"Does Christine know about my brother's death?"

"Yes, as does his son, Michael."

"Oh please, Paulo. Can we spend a few days in England after the cruise? I'd love to see Christine and Mikey – we got on so well, and then they stopped communicating when she left him."

Rachel felt it best that the reason for the marriage breakup come from Christine Jones, not from her.

"Have you tried to contact your brother since you've been on board?"

"I've asked a few of the waiters in the buffet when Paulo hasn't been there, but none of them seemed to know him."

Rachel thought that was odd, but said nothing.

"I will agree to stay in London for five days after the cruise, and then we must fly home. I have to get back to the business and sign papers to seal the deal. Now I think we have taken up enough of this young woman's time. Shall we go?"

"Who will arrange the funeral?" Stella looked at Rachel again.

"I'm sorry, I don't know," answered Rachel, thinking it would be unlikely that Michael or Christine would want to foot the bill for their estranged father/husband's final farewell. "I expect it might be covered by insurance. I'll ask Dr Bentley for you."

Paulo helped his wife to her feet and led her out of the office. Rachel hoped neither of them was involved in the demise of Stefan Sosa. It appeared they had suffered enough at his hands already. At least Stella had.

# Chapter 17

Rachel joined Sarah and her parents for dinner in the Club Restaurant. The restaurant was brightly lit with Christmas decorations and busy, but not full, so it gave her the opportunity to observe the waiters in a new light, knowing some of the secrets they were hiding.

She saw Mishka for what he was: a sneaky drug dealer who resented Stefan Sosa for blackmailing him over the issue. If it had been hard drugs, he would be at the top of her list because of the sums of money involved, but a small cannabis smuggling operation, though unwelcome on board a cruise ship, was not big enough to make him a drug baron, or anything like it.

She also noticed for the first time how Mishka shunned Danielle and snapped at her when out of earshot of diners. Obviously he believed Danielle had told Sosa his secret and had it in for her. Pash continued his avoidance technique whenever he was near their table. He charmed the Bradshaws with his bright white smile, but blanked Rachel – not that she minded. Her only interest in him was as a suspect; she had no wish to be his friend, but it did make it more difficult to find out anything from him. She had an idea who would be good at pumping him for information and would discuss it with Sarah and Jason once the Bradshaws busied themselves with other activities.

"Rachel, you're doing it again!" Mary chided while staring in her direction.

"What? Oh sorry, I was miles away." Rachel smiled meekly.

"That young man of yours has a lot to answer for, going away and leaving you at this time of year. I shall be having words when I next see him. It's not right, I can see how disappointed you are. When will you men learn?"

Mary's stern look was now directed at the gentle Gilbert Bradshaw, who sensibly continued eating. Rachel felt confused for a moment before realising that Mary had wrongly assumed she was still missing Carlos. The thought brought her up with a start.

*Why am I not missing him?*

Thankfully she had to park the question. Mary Bradshaw was in full flow on the topic of young love, but Sarah and Jason were now the ones high on her radar. Sarah reddened under the pressure and chewed her bottom lip, a habit she had when under stress and one that Rachel had always picked up on at university when they shared accommodation. At least Sarah was holding her tongue and not antagonising her mother.

"What are you doing after dinner this evening?" Rachel felt it was time to divert the conversation and her friend shot her a grateful glance.

Gilbert Bradshaw answered, "Mary had a visit to the hairdresser's this afternoon so I'm taking her to the indoor cinema. She always likes a treat after she's had her hair done, although why on earth she decides to waste an afternoon of our holiday in such a way when her hair looks perfectly respectable, I don't know."

"You know I have my hair done once a week come what may, Gilbert."

Sarah and Rachel laughed as it was a cause of some consternation in the Bradshaw home when a bank holiday dared to fall on a hairdressing day. Bank holidays were the only times when Mary deferred or brought forward her hairdressing appointments.

"Mum, you are funny. I hope you know you probably paid four times as much as having it done at home."

Mary blushed, and now it was she who changed the subject. "Your father had some gaming lessons in the casino and that's far worse than having a weekly hairdressing treat, if you ask me."

Following a period of friendly banter around the table, Sarah's parents left to head for the cinema. Rachel and Sarah opted to hang around and order tea while Rachel filled her friend in on the meeting with the Gonzalezes and the subsequent revelations. They roared with laughter, causing a few heads to turn, when Rachel described how she'd told Stella Gonzalez to 'go on'.

"You'll never forget that, will you? Bernard can be

such a card at times."

"His humorous interpretation of counselling did relax me enough to go in there, so I will have to thank him."

"Don't you dare! He'll be unbearable."

"Okay, I'll thank him in my head rather than out loud. Anyway, they were a nice couple, I thought, although Paulo could be a bit prickly. I sort of hope they're not involved in this, but I find it hard to believe that Stella at least hadn't been in contact with Sosa about the trip. It would surprise me if they hadn't arranged to meet up during this cruise. They did seem genuinely shocked about the death, though."

"What about Paulo? Do you believe he was unaware of his wife's contact with her brother and her intention to ask him to help recruit her nephew for financial help?"

"He was harder to read. He did put on a good show of being affronted at finding out, but he doesn't seem like the sort of man who wouldn't know what was going on in his own household. I would very much like to speak to both of them separately and see if either of them trips up. Stella appeared to be telling the truth for most of the time and relieved to be getting it out in the open. Having said that, the tears dried up quickly once she knew her husband's business was out of trouble, so her distress was more about money and not over her brother's untimely death, that's for sure."

"I don't think I can hold that against her, he was a ghastly man by all accounts. Even Bernard didn't like him and he likes everyone."

"As do you, Sarah Bradshaw, so if you don't feel sorry about Sosa's death, he must have been horrible. I haven't managed to dig up any redeeming features about his character from anyone."

"I wouldn't say I'm not sorry about his death, but perhaps the world won't miss him too much."

Mishka arrived with tea and began pouring for them.

"How are you, Mishka?" asked Sarah innocently.

"I'm well, nurse. I enjoyed our talk in Fátima yesterday and I have had no further problems with my eyes since you treated them." Mishka's face brightened; it was hard for anyone not to like Rachel's best friend, one of the kindest people on the planet as far as she was concerned.

"I expect you're all having to work extra hard since Stefan departed," Rachel spoke quietly, although they were not in earshot of any other passengers.

"We are, but it's a burden we are happy to bear to be rid of the man."

Mishka left them to drink their tea.

"Do you think it was him, Rachel?" Sarah whispered.

"No, I don't think so. A man so openly hostile doesn't go to the top of my list. Our killer would be more subtle, I believe. Having said that, maybe he doesn't have the brains to hide his feelings. Although some murderers play with you and almost challenge you to prove their guilt, and if that's the case he is highly intelligent. He's a paradox, though, isn't he? One minute he's having a religious experience, the next we find out he's a drug dealer!"

"Perhaps his religious experience will help him change his ways."

"You were at the meeting with Waverley. He sold drugs the day after his so-called spiritual revelation."

"It obviously wasn't a Damascus Road enlightenment, but that doesn't mean it wasn't real."

"My father always says that the proof of a religious experience is in the life that follows, otherwise it makes a nonsense of everything he teaches."

"Well, I wouldn't argue with Brendan Prince about theology, but back to the present. We're not doing very well with this one, are we? Jason's frantic with worry over Brenda's possible involvement. I do so hope it is one of the waiters."

"It could also be Claudia Kitova, who managed to keep herself under the radar until we found out she was also being blackmailed. We still don't know why. I was hoping you or Bernard could speak to her and find out."

"Already done, Sherlock. Jason asked Bernard to find out, and he only told me what he'd discovered tonight after surgery so Jason doesn't know yet. Apparently, the poor woman made the mistake of confiding in Sosa that she'd found a gold brooch belonging to a passenger and kept it. She felt guilty afterwards and asked his advice as to whether she would be fired if she handed it in a few weeks later. He told her yes, and then began blackmailing her."

"I do hope Waverley doesn't go after her, although she might have been desperate enough if Sosa tried to extort more money from her than she could afford."

"You're right, but she wanted to return the brooch, so she's honest underneath it all. I can't believe she would resort to murder."

"She does seem an unlikely candidate, but she was the last person to see him alive. Also he may have had something else on her that we haven't yet discovered."

"But wouldn't it be rather foolish to be the one to deliver his final meal, and then find the body afterwards?"

"Or very clever," said Rachel, rubbing her head, frustrated that she was no nearer to discovering Sosa's killer than before. "Changing the subject, Sarah, do you think there's something wrong with me?"

"What do you mean?"

"Twice now, your mother has assumed I've been missing Carlos when I haven't even been thinking about him. It makes me wonder whether I love him at all."

"Don't take any notice of Mum, you know what she's like. To her, love is everything. She sees romance under every bush – I blame Barbara Cartland."

Rachel laughed. "But surely I should be thinking about him."

"Rachel Prince, I've known you all my life, and when there's a puzzle to be solved, nothing and no-one gets in the way of it. Remember, we're different people to our parents. We don't hang on every word of the men in our lives, but it doesn't mean we don't love them. Mum's a romantic, she sees the world through a glass."

"Perhaps. I still have so many doubts over whether I can ever truly commit again."

"Rachel, if you don't stop harking back to the past, you won't ever move on. It's just plain fear, but you know in your heart of hearts that Carlos is the one for you. When did you last think of him?"

"When I woke up this morning. I even debated paying the hefty price for maritime roaming. If I had done, I might have saved myself from being attacked."

"Mm. There you are. You compartmentalise, Rachel. That's who you are and Carlos wouldn't want you any other way. It doesn't mean you don't love him, he knows that. If there wasn't a murder investigation going on, you'd most likely be pining away and running yourself to death up on deck sixteen."

They laughed at the reference to Rachel's keep fit fanaticism. "Well that's something I am missing. Perhaps I'm—"

"Go on!" said Sarah and they both burst into another giggling fit, preventing Rachel from saying whatever it was she had been about to say.

"Come on, let's get out of here before Pash throws us out," she said instead. The glare boring through the back of her head made her almost wish the new head waiter would turn out to be the killer. There were few people she disliked to any degree, but Pash was becoming one of them. She was convinced he would step into Sosa's shoes in every way and the waiters' current respite would soon be over. She had no doubt Pash would not be averse to a touch of blackmail himself, but perhaps she was just being unkind.

# Chapter 18

The familiar figure of CSO Jack Waverley loomed outside Rachel's stateroom when she returned.

"If it wasn't a cliché, I would say again we really should stop meeting like this, chief."

"I can only apologise, Miss Prince. May I come in?"

The seriousness in his tone and the 'Miss Prince' usage warned Rachel not to make any further wisecracks.

"Yes, of course."

Waverley followed her through to the sitting area and flopped down on the sofa.

"Drink?"

"Scotch please."

*Blimey, it must be serious.* Rachel poured a whisky from the mini bar and helped herself to a tonic water.

"What on earth's the matter?"

His right hand stroked through the receding hairline and the familiar cough preceded any attempt at conversation. He swallowed the whisky in one gulp.

"Brenda's gone missing. I don't know what to do."

"I think you had better explain what you mean by gone missing. It's quite difficult to go missing on the

*Coral*, but I don't need to tell you that. Is she not at work?"

"We had a row after I questioned her father. She got it in her head I didn't believe her when she told me she had nothing to do with Sosa's death. She's been on paid absence from the bakery since this business started; she's due back tomorrow."

"Could you not just reassure her that you do believe her? Assuming you do, that is."

"Of course I do, it's just that Richard's alibi for the hours before Sosa's death is that he went to his room to unpack, but nobody can confirm it. Also, he now admits he had a row with Sosa on the dockside. He denied it until I told him Goodridge had messaged to inform me that a passenger had identified him, and then both he and Brenda became defensive. I challenged Brenda about the short time she went missing from the bakery after cutting her finger and it all got out of hand. I left them to cool down while I met with Goodridge in my office. I've just been back to our room. She's packed a bag and disappeared."

"So she's not really gone missing; she's, erm, temporarily left you." Rachel tried to sound calm.

"I know what you're thinking. You think I should have stayed out of it and let Goodridge speak to them."

"Well it might have been less confrontational. You know you're too close to this, so yes, that would have been better, but there's not much point worrying about that now."

"What am I going to do? I think I should just leave her to calm down. Wait until the case is solved, then patch it up."

"And leave Brenda thinking forever that you don't trust her? No, you need to find her and convince her that you believe her *now* and that you were playing the role of bad cop, because that's what she would be likely to face from anyone else, and you'd rather it came from you. Then you need to apologise."

"But I didn't do anything wrong."

"Chief, what's more important to you? Your pride or getting your wife back?"

He smiled for the first time since entering the room. "You're wise beyond your years, Rachel Prince. I'm terrified of losing her; it scares me so much, it hurts. What would I ever do if she is involved?"

"I don't believe that, neither do you. Richard Jones may have come aboard to warn Sosa to stay away from his family, but do you seriously believe either he or Brenda could be involved in this? Also why would she implicate herself and the bakery? There's no way she would have known when Sosa would order food."

"But it wasn't in the food."

"Nevertheless, if she had known about the substance in the whisky, she would have somehow delayed his meal so the galley would play no part in the investigation. I'm sure your wife is intelligent, implicating herself would have been stupidity. The meal was ordered by coincidence.

"I also don't have your wife or father-in-law – not that I know him – down as cold-blooded killers. The more I think about it, the more I don't believe it's them – if they had killed him, it would have been a spur of the moment thing, not in this calculated fashion. And it was such a cruel way to kill someone, he must have been in agony."

"You're right. I knew it anyway, but thank you, Rachel, I'm convinced."

"Now you'd better go and convey that conviction to your wife and father-in-law. Don't let this fester."

Waverley hesitated. "I'll ask you about your progress tomorrow, but for now, I need to find my wife. She can't have gone far."

Rachel heaved a sigh of relief after he left and hoped she was right in her judgement that Richard and Brenda were truly innocent of any crime. Now it was time to work out her next steps.

Usually she would go to the gym and mull things over during a workout, but her hip was still sore from the stitches and she didn't want them to come apart. It was frustrating not being able to exercise as this was her go-to relaxation method. Perhaps some music would help.

She picked up her iPhone and noticed there was a message from Carlos. There must have been a temporary signal again. Her heart leapt when she read it.

*Case almost solved, hope to join ship on one of the Canary stops.*
*Will let you know when confirmed. Jason says I can bunk in with*
*him.*

Now she was far too excited to concentrate on suspects and murder. Carlos would be joining the ship in time for Christmas; she couldn't wait to let Sarah know, unless Jason had already told her. There was no signal on her phone to send a reply, but she picked up the stateroom phone and dialled her friend's number.

"Hello."

"Guess what?"

"You've heard then." Sarah giggled. "I wanted to tell you over dinner as I knew already, but Jason wouldn't let me. He said it was down to Carlos to tell you. I'm so pleased, Rachel. We're going to have a wonderful Christmas now. My parents will be over the moon."

"Nice that someone doesn't know before me."

"It's not like that. I was with Jason in Waverley's office, before I met you and my parents, when the call came through. Carlos wanted to check he would have somewhere to stay before getting your hopes up, and Jason had to get approval from the captain. Guest services contacted head office and they will add him as Jason's guest to join the ship as soon as we know when he's coming. We can't just let anyone walk on board a fully booked ship, you know."

"Oh, I should have thought of that, of course you

can't. Is Jason alright about it?"

"He's fine. He likes Carlos and was used to sharing with a lot more people in the army. Anyway he's got a sofa bed in his room. The two of them will be talking late into the night – sometimes I think men are worse than women when it comes to gossip."

"I can't thank Jason enough. This will be the best Christmas ever. Until I received the text message, I think I was shutting off my emotions; I was so disappointed not to be having our planned time together, I went into shutdown."

"I know that, Rachel. It was obvious to me – remember, I can read you. I recognised the signs."

"Why didn't you say something?"

"I almost did when you were worrying about your feelings earlier, but sometimes you have to work it out for yourself. Actually, I'm hoping Carlos will be a good influence on Jason. He might be able to get him to open up about Afghanistan and his own commitment issues."

"Do you want me to ask him to try?"

"No, I don't want Jason to think I'm manipulating things behind the scenes. That's the last thing he needs. I would rather it came naturally, otherwise neither of them will be relaxed."

"You're right. Carlos doesn't do contrived. I do hope he's right about solving his case within the next few days. If so, he's worked really quick, but I'm not complaining."

"I expect he had added motivation."

They laughed and chatted for a while longer before Sarah turned serious.

"There is just one thing. Carlos is not going to be happy that you have become embroiled in another case on board ship, and even less happy about your injuries."

"Good point. We need to get this case solved before he joins us and my wound needs to heal quickly. There's nothing like a deadline to get me going. That reminds me, I forgot to tell you about Waverley's visit."

"Oh?" Sarah sounded concerned.

"No, it's not like that. He wasn't warning me off for a change, although I'm sure that will come again – you know what he's like."

Rachel explained about the row he'd had with Brenda and his father-in-law and how Brenda had walked out.

"Oh dear. I do hope he can smooth things over. Trust is so important in a relationship." The wistful tone didn't escape Rachel's notice. She took a deep breath.

"Sarah, Jason loves you. Whatever has happened in his past, the two of you will work it out together. I have to believe that otherwise there's no hope for me and Carlos either."

"I hope so, Rachel, for all our sakes. For my part, there's always something missing because I know that Jason finds it so difficult to completely commit. It must be hard for Carlos. Perhaps you and Jason should talk and me and Carlos can console each other over our half-hearted lovers."

Rachel laughed loudly. "Now there's a thought. Of course it could be worse – if you and Carlos were together it would be too perfect, and if me and Jason were together we'd be forever in doubt. My father always says that relationships are based on joint respect and hard work once the passion has levelled out."

"He should know. Your parents make it work and your dad does enough marriage counselling to be an expert on the subject."

"He is, and I get what he means just as long as he doesn't try to counsel me."

"He wouldn't dare, but he'd be the first one I'd go to for pre-marital counselling if Jason ever gets around to asking me to marry him. At least you said yes when Carlos asked."

"I did, but he asked at the right time. There will be a right time for Jason. Oh Sarah, I've just realised what you said! That means you're ready to marry if he asks. You've always said you're not ready."

Rachel heard the giggle through the phone. "Well now I'm ready. I'm almost sorry because Mum will think it's her nagging that's got me here and I won't be able to deny her the satisfaction of believing it even though it's not true."

"Your mum means well, Sarah. She loves you, so stop moaning."

"I know, we get on great as long as there's a little distance between us, otherwise she wants to take complete control over everything. Dad just lets her dictate the terms of their marriage, but I don't want to be like that."

"But they are happy. Your dad adores her and vice versa. Mums only want daughters to be happily married and taken care of. Mine does anyway. Dad would be happy for me to be an independent single for life, but Mum wants me settled down and probably out of the police force."

"At least that's rational. I sometimes want you out of the police force, Rachel. It's so dangerous."

"Now you're sounding like your mother!"

They laughed again and said goodbye, arranging to meet the next morning on shore. They were going on a private tour of the island of Madeira, a Christmas treat from the Bradshaws.

Rachel felt the familiar fluttering in her stomach at the thought of seeing Carlos, but she needed to focus on getting this case solved. Still she hadn't found the time or the memory to mention the McCauleys to anyone. She hoped her theory about them not being in any danger until the return journey was right, but she was taking a huge risk.

# Chapter 19

The visit to Madeira had been a welcome break and the enforced rest in the people carrier helped Rachel's aches and pains ease off substantially. They had visited all the popular tourist attractions, including some areas off the beaten track. The weather had been warm and sunny.

"I can't believe it's December and we're only four days away from Christmas, it feels like summer." Mary Bradshaw had thoroughly enjoyed the island, and witnessing her pleasure had made everyone's day so much richer.

"Your mum's like a child again," Rachel had remarked to Sarah when they had stopped for lunch.

Sarah had beamed. "I love it when she's like this, she can be so happy and carefree when she lets go. Dad's enjoying it too, but he isn't an extrovert."

By the time they arrived back at the ship, they were all tired and Sarah had to rush off to get ready for surgery; she was also doing the on call. The medical and nursing staff took turns having days off and they were each having two days out of the next four on a rota, so Sarah would be off when they got to Gran Canaria. Bernard had also had the day off today, but had chosen to go to the beach with a group of Filipino friends.

Rachel said goodbye to the Bradshaws and made her way back to her room to get ready for dinner. The only problem with the day had been her dread of this evening's meal. An early morning telephone call from Dr Bentley had surprised her, and when he'd told her he had arranged for her to dine with Stella and Paulo Gonzalez that evening, she had not been at all happy.

Under Waverley's direction, Dr Bentley had encouraged the couple to attend, explaining that an informal conversation over a meal might help them move forward following the untimely death of their estranged relative. He had also managed to convince Stella that it was ship procedure to have a counselling session following a bereavement and that it could be informal or formal. Rachel was not keen to be an undercover counsellor again and had made that clear, but Dr Bentley told her it had all been Waverley's suggestion. Not wanting to upset the CSO in case he hadn't managed to patch things up with Brenda, she'd reluctantly agreed. The only advantage was that dinner was in the Steak Restaurant and the usual financial supplement was being waived.

Both Paulo and Stella knew how to dress, Rachel observed. From what she remembered of Stefan, he had been quite a scruffy looking man and totally unattractive, nothing like his elegant sister who turned men's heads with ease. Rachel was used to men looking at her because of her natural beauty, but it appeared that the fifty-year-old Stella Gonzalez could outdo her. She was happy about it as she never invited the attention and certainly didn't welcome it. As a woman, she appreciated glamour when she saw it, and the beautiful mature woman who joined her in the bar before they went through for dinner exuded glamour.

Rachel's beauty wasn't lost on Paulo, however, and she couldn't fail to detect a leer, not to mention the smell of alcohol not quite drowned out by strong aftershave, when he kissed her on the cheek on meeting. Stella appeared oblivious, but Rachel would keep Paulo at arm's length. When the waiter pulled out a chair so that Paulo could sit next to her at the table, Rachel declined.

"I prefer the view from here," she said as she moved to the chair next to Stella. The waiter hurried around the table and pulled out her preferred chair. Rachel noticed a twitch of a smirk on Paulo's lips. He was playing with her.

Paulo was given the wine list to choose drinks. Queen Cruises, like many cruise liners Rachel imagined, had not yet come to terms with the fact that women were quite capable of choosing their own drinks.

*At least they have moved on from asking men to order dinner for us*, Rachel thought. She was feeling irritable at having to keep up the counselling charade, and now she had to spend time with a man who had clearly had a little too much to drink. The consoling factor was that it might loosen his tongue, but she hoped he wouldn't be inappropriate and embarrass either her or his wife.

"What would you like to drink, darling?" Paulo handed the drinks menu to his wife and Rachel kicked herself for assuming he was a misogynist like his brother-in-law had been. Stella scanned it before handing it to Rachel.

"Would red be okay with you?" she asked.

"Yes, I'll be having steak, so red is superb. I don't mind which, you choose," Rachel replied, handing back the menu to Stella.

"Are you allowed to drink on duty?" asked Paulo, giving Rachel a penetrating gaze.

"As this is an informal conversation, it's allowed."

"Ah yes, an informal though compulsory meeting." He frowned.

"Don't start that again, Paulo. We're here for our own benefit, so try to be polite and enjoy dinner." Stella lifted her eyes to hold his. "Please, for my sake."

"Of course. I apologise, Miss Prince. I take it the Miss is correct, although not for too much longer, I see."

Noticing he was staring at her engagement ring, she blushed, and felt the blush deepening at the excitement of knowing that Carlos would be with her soon.

"It's Rachel, please. We don't need to be formal, as I've already said."

Paulo made to say something, but changed his mind

after a glare from his wife. The wine waiter arrived and looked towards Paulo, who directed him with a swift head movement to his wife.

"We'll have a bottle of Cabernet Sauvignon."

"Good choice, ma'am," said the waiter.

"Red wine is poor quality in Cuba. We have to import decent wine to drink, so I always bring some home when I go to the United States on business," explained Paulo to Rachel. "Cabernet Sauvignon is my wife's favourite with steak. I'll have a rum and coke," he added, turning to the waiter. "Just the two glasses for the wine."

Rachel wished Sarah was here; her friend loved steak, whereas Rachel could only take red meat in small quantities, and nerves were making her appetite disappear. If she had been with Sarah, there would have been no problem and a T-bone would be at the top of her list, but impersonating a counsellor was not enabling her gastric juices to flow.

They ordered dinner while their drinks were being poured and Rachel settled for a small sirloin, medium to well done. Paulo ordered a T-bone steak and Stella joined the sirloin fraternity. The Gonzalezes were quiet, waiting for Rachel to start her probing.

*Come on, Prince, pull yourself together or this evening is going to be a disaster.*

With that internal cajoling and a larger than usual sip of wine, she relaxed. What was the worst that could happen?

"This cabernet is delicious. I think I could get to like it." She had just managed to stop herself saying she might buy some when she got home.

Paulo nodded approval at her good taste as he wiped a piece of fluff off his jacket.

"Please tell me about Cuban cuisine. I'd love to hear more about your country."

"My mother was a wonderful cook," said Stella. "I'm not such a good cook and we hire someone who prepares most of our meals, except when it's a special occasion, then I do it. Our meals are a mix of Spanish and Caribbean. There is also an African influence on what we eat. We like spicy food, but not as hot as in Africa. The Americans like to feel they influence our tastes, but not really."

Stella told Rachel about some of her mother's home-made recipes that the family loved to eat and it wasn't long before she was feeling hungry. Rachel steered away from politics as she feared Paulo might not be easily controlled on that topic.

As the conversation and the alcohol flowed, both Paulo and Stella relaxed. Rachel was careful to drink slowly and cover her glass when the waiter came to refill, ensuring that Stella got the lion's share. Paulo had no problem requesting more rum and asked for separate bottles of coke so that he could choose how much to add. As he'd obviously started drinking early, he was soon speaking freely and unguardedly. Rachel sensed it was time to probe.

"Have you ever cruised before?" she asked.

"I used to join my brother for holidays aboard the *Coral Queen* when he first got a job as waiter. Paulo was never interested, but my parents came a couple of times until the relationship soured."

"What caused it to go sour?"

"It started after Stefan got divorced. My parents were Catholic and did not approve of divorce. They were devastated at not being able to see their grandson. Paulo and me couldn't have children." A tear threatened to fall, but with a blink of the eye it disappeared.

Paulo took over. "I didn't like Stella's brother, he was not a gentleman. I saw the way he treated his wife on the few occasions we met during holidays. The boy didn't seem happy. There were times when I wanted to snatch him away, I can tell you. That man didn't deserve to have a child while we—"

"Don't, Paulo. Anyway, my father was always the kindest of men and he loved my mother. I think Stefan was more like my uncle. He was the Cuban stereotype: male chauvinist, and this is what my mother didn't like. I think the divorce broke her heart and she became frail, ageing rapidly.

"The final meeting I mentioned yesterday between my parents and Stefan was devastating. At a family gathering, he blamed Mother for the breakup of his marriage, which was incorrect and unfair, but sadly she believed it and never recovered."

"We know who was responsible. You all protected him for too long, he was spoilt." Paulo turned to address Rachel. "Cuban boys, particularly oldest boys, are treated like you British treated your boys in the nineteenth century, Miss Prince. Sorry, Rachel." At this point, Paulo put a hand on his wife's shoulder. "Stella believed her brother could change, but trust me, he would never have changed. I can't pretend I'm sorry he's dead."

"What about you, Stella?"

"Paulo's right, I used to think Stefan could change and that he would one day come to his senses. After Father's death, when I saw that he had cost us our inheritance, I hated him for that. If I'd seen him then, I don't know what I would have done, but then I thought it could be the opportunity to bring those of us left closer together. I imagined he was close to his son because he'd always told the family that he was, but he tormented my parents, saying that his ex-wife would never let them see Mikey again. He was a cruel man, Rachel, I realise that now, and he lied to us all for years, so no, I am not sorry he's dead. I'm sorry he wouldn't change, but it seems it wasn't only his family he treated badly."

"What makes you say that?"

"There must have been a reason for someone to murder my brother. People don't kill for nothing. All I want now is to reconcile our friendship with Christine and Mikey. Mikey will be the only one left who can carry on the family name; there are no other Sosas left."

Rachel felt it best not to mention that Christine had changed the boy's surname back to her family name, or that there was also a daughter who could carry on the bloodline, if not the name. Danielle Barcellos would most likely prefer not to become acquainted with Stefan's family, even if they did appear genuine. If everything they were saying was true, the Gonzalezes could be relegated to the bottom of her suspect list, and while she was pleased, it was frustrating not knowing who was responsible for Sosa's death.

The meal ended with coffees all round, and despite Paulo's initial guardedness, he and Stella both admitted they had had a wonderful evening and felt they had made a new friend. Rachel wasn't sure whether it was the drink talking, but she had warmed to the couple and empathised with how the family had suffered at the hands of the late Stefan Sosa.

If only she wasn't driven by the desire to see justice done, she would forget about the case, but that's not who she was.

# Chapter 20

Rachel woke with renewed vigour. Now she had ruled out the Gonzalez couple it was time to refocus on the chief suspect in her mind, Pashmarli Bakshi. With the inheritance ruled out as a motive, he had the most to gain from Sosa's death.

After going for a gentle gym workout and steering clear of the running track, she ate breakfast in the buffet and waited for Bernard and Sarah to join her.

"Good morning, Rachel. You even look beautiful in the morning, how can that be?" Bernard arrived first, and Sarah followed a few minutes later.

"What's this all about?" she asked.

"I've more or less ruled out Stella and Paulo Gonzalez."

"The subterfuge worked then?"

Rachel scowled at Sarah. "Not that I liked it one little bit, but yes it did. They had quite a lot to drink and that loosened their tongues. They are easy to read, and although there was no love lost between Stella and her brother, she is a kind person at heart."

"Ah, but what about him? Slimy looking fella, I

thought."

"Bernard, stop it," said Sarah.

"No, he is a trifle smarmy, but underneath it all, he appears to love his wife and I don't believe he knew Sosa still worked on board this ship, whereas Stella did. I still don't have her down as a murderer, though."

"But you said there was no love lost between Stella and her brother, and money is often behind murder."

"My gut tells me she didn't do it."

The three laughed loudly. Rachel's gut was something that annoyed Waverley to distraction and he often rebuked her over her intuition.

"So who did do it then? We need to find out before Carlos joins the ship," said Sarah.

Bernard's eyes widened. He was clearly not included in the people who were in the know about Rachel's fiancé coming on board.

"That's wonderful news. When?"

"He hasn't confirmed yet, it will either be tomorrow in Gran Canaria, or more likely Lanzarote on Christmas Eve," Rachel answered.

"I am so pleased. I only met him on your first cruise and that seems a lifetime away. I wish my family could join us, but not to be."

"I'm sorry, Bernard. You must miss them at this time of year."

"I do, but I will be on leave again soon enough. We will Skype on Christmas Day and I get to watch them open their presents." A tear threatened to fall as Sarah patted him on the shoulder.

"You're with your second family. Not quite the same, but we'll have fun."

Bernard smiled at his colleague, and then returned his attention to Rachel with quizzically raised eyebrows.

"Back to our murder suspects. Okay, Pash is my chief suspect. He had opportunity, and he has motive once we put the inheritance money to one side. He's ambitious and wanted to take over as maître d; he hated Sosa because he was being blackmailed; and he knew about his boss's drink habit. It would have been easy for him to spike the whisky anytime during the day when Sosa was off ship."

Sarah was making warning signals with her eyes and frantically pointing with her head. Rachel stopped speaking and looked behind her to find Waverley smirking with raised eyebrows.

"Do go on, don't mind me," he said and sat down next to Rachel.

"Anyway, Bernard, I can't get anything out of him. Pash won't speak to me, so I thought you might be able to take him to the crew bar or wherever he hangs out after work and gently grill him. See if you can get him to open up about his life; I'm sure he's itching to tell someone how much he hated the dead man."

Bernard rubbed his hands together. "Yippee! I finally get to use my detective skills."

"You've already used them twice on this voyage," Sarah reminded him.

"Oh yes, but that was easy." Looking at Rachel, he said, "Okay, I'll do it."

"Actually, you won't," said Waverley, causing them to protest in unison. "Stop! It's not that I won't allow it; it's just that, although the plan may seem like a good one, Miss Prince – and far be it from me to argue with your 'gut' – I'm afraid this time your radar is way off."

"What do you mean?" asked Sarah.

Rachel grimaced. "You've already arrested him."

"Wrong again. No, it appears that Pashmarli Bakshi has gone AWOL. A general search has revealed nothing."

"Why would he hide unless he thought you were on to him, Rachel?" Sarah asked.

"Either that or I am wrong and he's become a second victim," Rachel muttered before pouring herself another strong coffee from the pot on the table. "In which case, we're back to square one and are no nearer to finding the killer. What do you think?" Rachel addressed her question to Waverley, who appeared to be enjoying her consternation.

"It's hard to tell. He could be our man and someone found out and threatened him so he's gone into hiding, or – and I'm more inclined to believe this – he is another victim, as you suggest."

"When was he last seen?"

"He finished up in the Club Restaurant yesterday

evening and went to the crew café afterwards and hasn't been seen since. His roommate Bruno Marks, erm, bunked down with a member of steward staff overnight while her roommate worked the nightshift." Waverley's face reddened. "These things do go on; they are consenting adults, after all. His story has been confirmed by the room steward, Arlene Fernandez."

Rachel smiled at Waverley's discomfort and Sarah scolded him. "Chief, what century did you come out of? We're not embarrassed."

Waverley coughed. "Quite. Anyway, Bakshi's bed hasn't been slept in so we suspect he didn't go back to his room. Bruno Marks says nothing is missing as far as he can see. He confirms that Pash does stay out overnight sometimes as he has a girlfriend on board. Of course we know who that is now. It's a pity her husband doesn't because everyone else seems to, poor man."

"Have you asked the girlfriend?" Rachel prompted before Waverley went into a tirade about marital infidelity. She knew that his first wife had left him for his best friend and it had taken him a long time to get over it and marry Brenda.

"Goodridge managed to discretely speak to her this morning. She says she hasn't seen him in that way since the ship sailed. Was most put out about it, according to Goodridge. I'd like to—"

"So where could he have got to?" Rachel steered him again.

"We don't know. Ravanos and Goodridge are going through CCTV footage of the ship's perimeter from the time he was last seen until now, just in case he was drunk and fell overboard, or killed himself."

"I see. How long is that likely to take?"

"It could take all day, depends if there's anything to find. I hate tying my officers up like this; it's a laborious task unless they get lucky."

Waverley's radio sprang into life with loud crackles. He pressed a button.

"You'd better come down, sir." Jason's voice was just about recognisable through the radio intercom.

"I need to go."

"I'm coming with you," said Rachel.

"What about your outing?" called Sarah.

"Please call your parents and apologise, tell them my hip's sore after the trip yesterday. Sorry, speak later."

Sarah nodded. "Okay I'll tell them you'll take a walk locally after you've rested."

"If that's settled, let's go."

Waverley marched off at a pace with Rachel following swiftly behind.

Although Rachel had been into Waverley's office many times, she had not been in the security office where the CCTV footage was recorded and from where the rest of the security team carried out their work behind the scenes. It reminded her of a CID room with monitors, computers and notice boards where crimes were listed.

She couldn't resist glancing at the operations board and noticed that murder wasn't the only crime being investigated by the security team.

There was a contraband liquor investigation, a poisonous spider smuggled aboard by a crew member and an assault on a passenger by another passenger in the launderette. The offending passenger was down to be escorted off-ship today; his family members were staying on board and he would have to make his own way home. Two crew members had gone AWOL in Southampton and details had been handed to the British immigration department, and there were photos of people wanted by Interpol to the right-hand side.

Waverley tapped her on the shoulder. "As you can see, we don't twiddle our thumbs all day, Rachel. This is a big ship and opportunists try to take advantage."

"I did realise you dealt with crimes, but didn't know just how many," she said.

"Why would you? We pride ourselves on keeping the ship secure and solving crime as quickly as possible. As well as solving crimes, we do our best to be a presence that prevents them. Some petty stuff like passengers hiding an extra bottle of alcohol in their luggage, we ignore, but we take safety of passengers and crew very seriously, which is why we will be dealing with Mishka Prostakov as soon as this murder is solved. Right, let's see what we have."

Rachel followed the chief of security to where Jason

was waiting for them.

"This footage was recorded at 2am, sir." Jason pressed play and they watched the edge of the ship under infrared lighting. The screen was labelled 'crew pool', and as the camera rolled a fuzzy figure came into view.

"Unfortunately we only scour the perimeter to see if anyone has gone overboard; the actual crew pool is not monitored. Crew need their privacy," Waverley explained.

The footage played on and the man in the picture could be seen going overboard.

"Can you tell if it's Pash?" Rachel asked.

"Rewind and zoom in, Goodridge."

Jason did as was requested. Although the image wasn't clear, she recognised the shocked face of the man falling as Pash.

"Are you thinking what I'm thinking?" she asked.

"Yes, he went over backwards, so it appears from this angle he was pushed – hard. Try a 360 degree turn."

Jason did so and another person could be seen, pushing the unfortunate Pash overboard.

"Get in closer."

"We can't, sir. The 360 doesn't zoom and the other cameras on that perimeter wouldn't pick it up."

"Blast! Now we have two murders. Have you informed the coastguard and given coordinates?"

"Yes, sir."

"Does he have any chance?" Rachel knew the answer, but wanted to ask anyway.

"Not an iota. With cold Atlantic currents reducing the night-time temperatures and the added fact he would have hit the water at speed, he would either have died on impact or within minutes. Heart attack, most likely."

Rachel looked at the screen again and noticed the blackness of the water; it made her shudder. As much as she hadn't liked Pash, no-one deserved to die like that. Her legs turned to jelly and she wondered if she might faint.

"Are you alright, Rachel?" asked Jason.

"Just felt a bit weak for a moment. Do you mind if I sit?" Jason helped her to a chair and brought her a glass of water. "Sorry, I'm not often squeamish, but the thought of someone going into the water like that—"

"Are you having flashbacks to your first cruise?" asked Waverley. She nodded and neither of them said anything else on the subject.

"We need to find out who's doing this and why. I'm at a loss," she said.

Ravanos excused himself to go back to work and Waverley and Jason pulled up chairs. The atmosphere was glum. It was one thing knowing people went overboard, but another watching it a few hours later on CCTV. Rachel realised that this would not have been the first time the security staff had watched such footage, and a new admiration for them and their work settled itself within her mind.

"Looks like we're back to the galley maid if it wasn't

Pash, unless you can shed any light on the Gonzalez couple?"

"I had dinner with them last night, as per your instructions, and either I'm becoming gullible or they are innocent. I don't see them being up for it, nor having time to get to Sosa's room and spike his drink. They do have motive, in that Sosa had caused the family much pain, but their intention as far as their nephew is concerned seems restorative rather than malicious."

Waverley coughed. "I've managed to smooth things over with Brenda and Richard and I don't think we need to be concerned on that front. Now I have the dilemma of whether to let them know about Mikey's aunt and uncle being on board. At least I will have, once these murders have been solved."

Rachel nodded, wondering whether the Gonzalezes would be at all welcome as far as the Jones family was concerned, but that was something she didn't need to burden herself with.

"So who's left? We have your chief suspect, Claudia Kitova—"

"Who had motive and opportunity," reinforced Waverley.

"Agreed. Then there's Mishka Prostakov, who also had motive and opportunity. Perhaps you should delve deeper into his drug dealing and check whether he is involved with more than cannabis?"

"Thank you for the suggestion, Rachel. We would

never have thought of that."

Ignoring the sarcasm, Rachel continued, "Sacha Voronin had opportunity, but as far as we are aware, no motive, and finally Danielle Barcellos, who also had motive and opportunity. But her motive is not enough to commit murder and she appears to have been able to manage Sosa's demands and manipulate him in her own way. I don't think she really believed he wanted contact with his daughter any more than he wanted amicable contact with his son, whom he had abused."

"So, of those four, we can exclude Voronin, although I suggest you look into him, Goodridge, and check we haven't missed anything. The strongest motive lies with Prostakov and Kitova. My money's on Kitova because we can pin her down to the exact crime scene and she was the one who felt she had the most to lose for pocketing a passenger's brooch. I've done some digging and the woman is a widow with three young children who live with the grandmother in Romania. They are poor, on the breadline in fact, and she sends all her wages home every month to feed and school them."

"And yet she was going to confess and hand the brooch back in? Poverty doesn't make her a killer."

"No, poverty doesn't, but there are two things you're missing, Rachel. Firstly, we only have her word that she wanted to hand the brooch back, and even if that was true, desperation could have forced her into murder. And that woman is desperate to keep her job."

"What would have happened if she had handed in the brooch?"

"It's difficult to say. That would have been up to her manager and it would depend on her work record and previous strikes. I suspect she would have got a severe reprimand and a warning, but it would be a harsh person to sack her for yielding to temptation in her situation and then finding a conscience."

"That makes it all the more cruel that the wretched Sosa blackmailed the woman and lied to her." Jason gritted his teeth, his jaw set with indignation. The more she got to know him, the more Rachel liked Jason. He was a kindred spirit, one who searched for justice and hated bullies.

"Then I sincerely hope it wasn't her," she said as she left the two men to their work.

# Chapter 21

Rachel decided to leave the ship and take a walk outside to get some fresh air. It was another lovely day with a clear blue sky and bright sunshine. How different to how it must be in England at this time of year.

Santa Cruz de la Palma was the first Canary Island stop, on the island of La Palma. Normally, Rachel would have been excited and keen to explore, but a man had just died and she was struggling to erase the image of the shocked face of Pashmarli as he went overboard. That, coupled with the guilt at not having liked the man, left her feeling morose – a mood that she was not altogether familiar with.

Carlos would be with her tomorrow or Christmas Eve, and the flutter of excitement that filled her stomach temporarily took her mind away from this latest murder. As she braced herself against a brisk but not unpleasant wind, in spite of rising temperatures, she pulled on a light jumper.

She walked steadily, but was still aware of the pulling of stitches to her right hip and pain from the bruising and the kick to the ribs. Her hands were healed now, which was a relief. Arriving at a bench facing out to sea, she stopped to rest and enjoy the wind blowing across her hair.

She had been almost convinced that Pash had murdered Sosa and would now be taking over his nasty work. Her bias against a man who had shunned her sat uncomfortably. Perhaps she had been too tired to see clearly. A bit of self-reflection might do her good at this moment, because her radar had been well off due to a petty dislike.

Now that they had to find out who'd killed Sosa and Pash, she wondered if there might be two killers. Could Pash have killed Sosa, and then someone else killed Pash? And why? For similar or altogether different reasons? She was beginning to think they might not get to the bottom of the investigation and the killer or killers might jump-ship. Not likely, though, if they thought they'd got away with it.

"Think, Prince, think!"

The wind was getting up so she decided to walk towards the town. The cobbled streets didn't make it easy for her hip, so she changed her mind and walked along the marina instead. The houses visible on the surrounding hills were bright and colourful from where she walked, a stark contrast to the mood she had been in not long before, but the walk was helping.

A short way along, she heard a sound coming from behind the end of a building. It sounded like someone was crying. She continued to walk the few paces past the obstruction of the building and recognised Danielle with her elbows leaning on a rail, her head buried in her hands.

Rachel walked over. "Are you alright?"

The young woman jumped. "Sorry, I didn't realise anyone was out here." Tears fell down her face and her eyes were puffy. She gathered herself together and wiped her eyes with a tissue before blowing her nose.

"I was just getting some fresh air, but decided not to go into town. I love the smell of salt blowing in from the sea when it's a windy day."

"I like fresh air too. When I go home, I walk for miles. It can be a long time cooped up on a ship."

"Yes, my friend Sarah says the same. She's always pleased to get home, but she keeps coming back to cruising so there must be something."

"There is. We make a lot of friends working on a cruise liner, they become like family. But it's been more difficult lately."

"Are you homesick?"

"A little. I have a daughter – I miss her so much, but she gets a good life and I earn more money here than I could back home."

"What's your daughter's name?"

"Rosa, she's seven."

"Does her father live at home?" Rachel knew this might scare her off, but she wanted Danielle to believe she wasn't aware of her past or the blackmail.

"No, he's dead. You're the friend of Nurse Sarah, aren't you? I've seen you with her and her parents in the Club Restaurant. I realise who you were talking about now."

"Yes, and you're the wine waitress. It's good to meet you properly. My name's Rachel."

"Danielle, although my friends call me Dani."

"Do you have a preference?"

"Dani, it makes me feel more at home. I'm sorry for crying, it's just that I have a lot on my mind at the moment."

"I'm a good listener if you want to talk."

"But you're a passenger."

"Think of me as a friend. We are all just people, aren't we? And you're off-duty, I see."

"Okay, it would be nice to talk to someone."

"Shall we get a coffee? There's a café up ahead."

Danielle agreed and they walked in silence towards the café on the quiet marina. Rachel ordered coffee.

"My treat, have whatever you want."

"Thank you, that's kind. I'll have black coffee, please."

Once the coffees had been brought to them, Rachel encouraged her.

"Right, Dani, please tell me what's on your mind, if you want to."

Dani took a sip of coffee and looked at Rachel, appraising her. "I've been so unhappy for a few years, and just when I think things are better, they have got worse again."

"How?"

"My daughter's father is – was a bad man. He caused me and a lot of other people a lot of harm. He worked on board the ship. I think I remember you saying you met him on the coach coming down from London."

"Oh, you mean the maître d who died from an allergic reaction?"

"Yes, him. Don't judge me, Rachel, but I was relieved when he died. I don't know what I ever saw in him. When I first came on board the ship, I was lonely and didn't know anyone. There were lots of cliques. Stefan was friendly, told me he was lonely too, that he was a long way from home and that he didn't have any friends. He said he would take care of me.

"One night, I had too much to drink. He encouraged it, but I just wasn't used to it. I found myself in his bed the next morning and thought, *what the heck?* After that we were together, but he became nasty, threatening. One day he hit me when I was seven months pregnant. That was it – I ended it."

"Did he try to get you back?"

"Yes, he tried nice, then he tried nasty, but I told him that if he came near me again in that way, I would report him. That seemed to do the trick because his boss didn't like him. I was safe for a while, but I was frightened for my baby. I told him she wasn't his and said I had slept with other men on board as well as him. He was angry, but believed it. But I decided to leave my daughter with my parents where she would be safe.

"I was always terrified that one day he would kidnap her, even though I told him she wasn't his. Deep down I think he knew she was and often threatened he would find her. It frightened me what he might do, but I don't believe he cared about her, or me. He wanted to have a hold over me so that I—"

Danielle stopped.

"So that you, what?"

"That doesn't really matter, but I have been happy for a few days, and now I'm back to the beginning."

"In what way?"

"I'm sorry. I can't say any more. I need to go back to ship and get ready for work. Please don't mention this if you see me in the restaurant."

"Of course not, but—"

"Sorry, thanks for listening." Danielle hurried away before Rachel could say anything else.

Rachel remained at the café and pondered the conversation for a while. She already knew the details about Stefan and how he had blackmailed Danielle and understood why she'd held that part of the story back, but what had spooked her now? Perhaps she was just homesick and missing her daughter.

Stefan would certainly not have made a good father as his treatment of Michael had demonstrated, so Danielle had done the right thing keeping her daughter away from him. Rachel wondered again whether to tell Danielle about Stella Gonzalez, but it wasn't her place to do so. The only explanation was that Danielle had become involved with another poor choice of boyfriend, or that someone had taken the place of Sosa on the blackmailing front.

Rachel made her way back to the ship to meet Bernard and Sarah for a late lunch.

The Bradshaws were back following a morning tour and they all met up in the Club Restaurant. Rachel was pleased when Brigitte, who had also been off ship, joined them. Bernard was on his best behaviour in front of Sarah's parents, in spite of Brigitte having the occasional dig trying to provoke a response. The three nurse friends laughed happily as they bantered, and Rachel joined in a few times.

Mary and Gilbert Bradshaw seemed happy to meet Sarah's friends and quizzed them about life on board a cruise ship.

"I'm sure Sarah doesn't tell us the worst, she paints a picture of being on permanent holiday," said Mary.

"I don't!"

"Well I can assure you it isn't," said Brigitte. "We work hard; even when we're off, we're on duty. We can get called to emergencies at all hours. Sometimes people—"

A kick under the table from Sarah prevented her revealing anything else.

"It can be busy, but we love the work. Mostly small things, nothing to worry about," said Bernard. "Brigitte's just miffed because I had to call her back to surgery last night to help me with a young child who wouldn't stop crying."

"Hm, I'm not surprised he cried, looking at you," retorted Brigitte.

"She was on a daaaate, that's why she's cross." Bernard sat back triumphantly, having got the last word with Brigitte – a rarity.

"See, Mum, Dad, this is what I have to put up with."

Even Mary Bradshaw laughed, although Rachel suspected a further interrogation would be in store for Sarah later.

"Where's that pleasant fellow gone? Pash, was it?" Gilbert Bradshaw asked.

A quick exchange of glances followed before Sarah answered, "He's gone down with something."

Rachel shot Bernard a warning look before he made some joke about Pash going overboard. He managed to control his mischievous grin, but couldn't resist adding, "Cold, I think."

"Oh well, the new man seems pleasant too. In fact, the service on board this ship is wonderful. We are really enjoying ourselves. I'm hooked."

"Well don't get too settled," warned Mary.

"Aren't you enjoying it, Mum?"

"Your mother is having a great time, but the motion has made her feel a bit unsteady at times. I think if we do another one, it will be a fly cruise, somewhere hot from the outset."

"Never mind me, Sarah. I am enjoying myself and there's so much to do. We loved Lisbon, and today's terra firma did me good. The sea days are nice, but I prefer solid ground beneath my feet."

"Well you've got another two days of terra firma ahead, so don't worry. Then you'll be looking forward to resting up again for the sail home. Are you going off ship again before we sail?"

"No, we might have an afternoon nap while the ship isn't moving."

"It's going to be a wonderful Christmas, darling." Gilbert Bradshaw took his wife's hand. "And Sarah and Jason have tomorrow off."

"Rachel has some news," said Sarah.

"Oh?" Mary and Gilbert both looked at Rachel.

"Carlos is expecting to finish his case and will be joining the ship tomorrow or the day after."

"Now that is good news. You've been a bit out of sorts for the past few days, and that fall didn't help. You're still limping." Mary gave Rachel a sympathetic smile.

"Yes, it has been a bit sore and I will be pleased to see

Carlos."

"Where's he staying? I thought the ship was fully booked."

"Don't worry, Mum. He's bunking in with Jason. Special permission from the captain."

Brigitte raised an eyebrow. She didn't comprehend Rachel and Sarah's views on celibacy before marriage and often chided Sarah about it. "You guys would have been better living in Victorian England. I don't know how your men put up with it."

"You mean without it," Bernard joked.

"Now, now, let's not lower the tone," said Mary, but even she couldn't resist a smile towards Bernard whose humour had got through to her.

Sarah changed the subject. "I'm off until evening surgery and the crew are rehearsing for their Christmas show soon. Would you like to come?"

"No, thank you. We want to see it live, and I really do want a nap. I haven't been sleeping very well," answered Mary.

"What about you, Rachel?"

"I'd love to, what time and where?"

"Four o'clock in the theatre."

The party finished their coffees and dispersed. Rachel had something else on her mind; something was bothering her about the will and she wanted to work out what it was before she joined Sarah in the theatre.

# Chapter 22

The Coral Theatre was packed with crew by the time Rachel arrived. The atmosphere was charged with tension. The crew occasionally got to perform for passengers, and as it was Christmas, they were even more determined to make it the best show ever. Sarah waved, beckoning her down to the front. Bernard was sitting next to her as they were not taking part in the entertainment, but were on first aid duty.

"This is just the rehearsal and you would think they were getting ready for an Oscar-winning performance. A lot of fuss if you ask me." Bernard grinned.

Sarah nudged him. "Shush, Bernard, someone will hear. Please don't upset them, they are working so hard to get it right."

Rachel relaxed in a seat the other side of Sarah and took in the scene, marvelling at the ornately decorated gold-coloured Christmas tree standing in the back corner of the stage. The ship was becoming more Christmassy as each day passed.

"Who's in charge?"

"Carla, the cruise director, but the real boss is

Graham," Sarah answered.

"Graham as in Dr Bentley?"

"Oh yes, he fancies himself as a theatre producer, setting himself up for retirement. Does this every year, and I have to say, the show is always the highlight of a Christmas cruise." Bernard grinned again.

"Be quiet down there," Graham called.

"He takes his role very seriously," whispered Sarah.

"I take it this is the *Babushka* rehearsal?" Rachel whispered back.

"Yep, then on the night there will be an acapella choir followed by well-known Christmas carols, and the passengers can join in with the singing if they want to."

"That should be fun. Does any of the crew abstain or object to the theme?"

"No, they love it, so unless they're working, in which case they do miss out, the majority are keen to be involved. The only arguing is about who plays who, but Carla and Graham have dealt with the divas."

Rachel sat back and enjoyed watching the crew act out the beautiful Russian folk story. The nativity play was one she had occasionally seen performed in her father's church as it served as a fun alternative to the traditional one, but this was the musical version of *Babushka* that could only be performed under licence.

The part of Babushka was being played by Brigitte, much to the amusement of Bernard, who roared with laughter at his friend and colleague playing an old woman who wouldn't believe that Jesus had been born.

"Grumpy, argumentative old woman suits her," he said mischievously.

The performance went to plan, apart from a few mishaps where people forgot their lines and some lighting issues. During the break, Rachel observed Mishka whispering something to Danielle. They were taking part in the play with minor roles, but Danielle seemed upset again and Mishka patted her on the shoulder before he was called away. Rachel suddenly worked out what it was she had been concerned about and it filled her with dread.

Jason joined them. "How's it going?"

"They're almost done. Graham's going to make them do it again to iron out a few problems. Rachel told us about Pash earlier."

Jason nodded, but didn't say anything else as there were too many people around. When the rehearsal started again, Rachel nudged Jason and whispered in his ear. He nodded again before getting up and leaving, much to the dismay of Sarah.

"What was that all about?"

"Just a hunch, he'll be back soon," Rachel reassured her friend.

Dr Bentley appeared pleased with the repeat performance and congratulated the crew on their dedication. He told them that final rehearsal would take place on Christmas Eve a couple of hours before the live performance, and then they could all relax.

Waverley arrived just as people were dispersing. Once the area was clear, he nodded at Rachel grimly.

"Goodridge has a copy of the will. It seems you were right. It's time to speak with Ms Barcellos. I've asked him to check the crime scene before we speak to her."

"What's going on, you two?" asked a disgruntled Sarah. Bernard stayed put, clearly wanting to be in the picture too.

Waverley coughed. "Rachel will tell you later. Now shall we go somewhere a little more private?"

Rachel gave Sarah an apologetic look and followed the chief down to his office. Once they were ensconced inside, he poured her a coffee from his percolator. A few minutes later, Jason arrived with Danielle.

"Please take a seat, Ms Barcellos," instructed Jason while he moved away to show something to Waverley that Rachel couldn't see. Waverley nodded, and then took a seat in one of the armchairs. Danielle stared at Rachel with fear-filled eyes.

"What's going on?" she asked.

"Ms Barcellos, is it true that Stefan Sosa was blackmailing you into stealing for him from the wine and drinks cellar?"

Danielle stared down at her hands and answered in the affirmative. "Is that what this is about? I told Bernard and gave him permission to report me, so I take it he has. I'm pleased to have it out in the open. Do what you will."

Ignoring her last remark, Waverley continued, "Did you then decide to get rid of your tormentor by spiking one of the bottles of whisky that you supplied while he was ashore on the day the ship was docked in Southampton?"

Danielle gasped. "No, how could you think such a thing? I didn't like him, I admit that, but I had no reason to kill him. I was able to manage him in my own way. I thought his death was an accident."

"You know full well that your ex-lover was murdered."

Rachel didn't like the way this interview was going, but kept quiet. Danielle's face reddened at the reference to her past and she looked at Rachel briefly.

"Stefan was not only blackmailing me. If it was murder, others had bigger reasons to get rid of him. Pash, Mishka and—"

"I will come on to Pashmarli Bakshi shortly, but for now I want an explanation for the first killing."

Danielle's head shot up. "What are you talking about, the first killing?"

"Don't play games with me, Ms Barcellos. Here, take a look at this, and then try and deny that you knew about it."

Waverley handed over a copy of the will that Rachel had asked Jason to retrieve from Stella Gonzalez. Danielle's hands shook as she read through the contents.

"So it is true?"

"You did know then?" Waverley pressed.

Danielle tightened her lips, frightened to say anything that might incriminate her any further, and shook her head with disbelief.

"Pash told you?"

"Told me what, Ms Barcellos?"

Danielle grabbed Rachel's hand. "I didn't do it. Pash told me about this will last night; he threatened that if I didn't share the money with him, he would tell security that I killed Stefan. He had seen me take a new bottle of whisky into Stefan's room on the day we left port. I swear I didn't put anything in the whisky, but Pash said someone killed Stefan and that everyone would believe it was me. Up until last night, I'd thought the death was from allergic reaction. People were saying nuts were in the bread that had been delivered to his room on the day we left Southampton. I was frightened, although I thought Pash was lying, but just in case, I agreed that if the will existed, I would give him money, even though I didn't kill Stefan."

Rachel asked, "Did Pash tell you how he knew about the will?"

"No, I wasn't even sure it existed."

Waverley cut in, "But you weren't satisfied with half the money for your daughter, were you? After arguing with him in the Club Restaurant last night – yes, you were seen – you followed Pash around for the evening, and in the early hours of this morning you threw him overboard."

Danielle's eyes widened. "What do you mean, threw him overboard? Is Pash dead?"

"Oh do come on, Ms Barcellos, don't play us for fools. You know full well he is dead, and not only that, you were the one who killed him. Officer Goodridge here found this in a sill where he went overboard."

Waverley threw a badge down on to the table, a look of smug satisfaction plastered on his face. Rachel picked it up: it was Danielle's name badge. Turning it around, she showed it to Danielle.

"I lost it last night. I took it off after the row with Pash to wipe a stain from my jacket. I must have put it on the drainer in the waiter-only area; I was upset and left in a hurry. Anyone could have picked it up. Please, I didn't do this."

"Very convincing story, Ms Barcellos. I give it to you that you tell a good yarn, but I'm not taken in for one moment. You are under arrest for the murders of Stefan Sosa and Pashmarli Bakshi. You will be taken to the brig and locked up to be returned to the authorities in Southampton on our return. Do you understand?"

Quiet sobbing was the only sound coming from Danielle. Her shoulders shook before she lifted her head and pleaded with Rachel.

"Please, I know how this looks, but I don't know who killed them. It wasn't me. I'm being framed. I have a daughter, I cannot go to prison for something I didn't do."

"Goodridge, take this woman away," ordered Waverley.

As soon as they left, Waverley laughed. "Thank goodness that's all over. Well done, Rachel, it was a good thing we checked the will and found the clause that the inheritance was to be shared with any surviving grandchildren. It's always about money, isn't it?"

Rachel sat quietly, weighing up all she'd heard over the past half hour. She had been convinced they had their killer, but her instinct was now telling her something was terribly wrong. How could she explain that to Waverley when all she had to go on was her gut?

"Rachel?"

"Sorry, I was elsewhere. I'm pleased for you that Brenda is now in the clear and that you have arrested someone."

"You're not having second thoughts, are you? Surely that little charade didn't fool you. She's guilty, Rachel; she had ample motive, ample opportunity, and both men threatened to take her daughter's inheritance away. I don't believe for one minute that she'd only just heard about the will. A court will convict her and I'm sure she'll confess soon enough."

"Who told you she was arguing with Pash last night?"

"Mishka Prostakov – don't look at me like that, Rachel. Just because the man was also being blackmailed by Sosa doesn't mean he isn't telling the truth. Anyway, you heard her admit to it."

"Yes, that's true, I heard her admitting to arguing with Pash last night. I hope we haven't got this wrong; she was shocked at the news of Pash's death, and she did openly admit that he threatened to put her in the frame for Sosa's murder."

"Only after she thought Pash had already told us."

"Why would she think that if she knew Pash was already dead?"

"I expect she thought she'd knocked him off before he told us and was genuinely shocked that he managed to get to us first."

"But why would she think he would do that if she'd agreed to give him the money?"

"Rachel, stop. It's her. We have the right person, now leave it alone. Go and enjoy the rest of your cruise. I for one won't be shedding any tears over a woman who goes about killing people over money. Nor, for that matter, for the two dead men. Sounds like they both had it coming, but that does not make their murders right. Leave it now, please. You heard what she said, and the evidence against her is compelling. It was her badge at the murder scene, and from her own mouth we now know that she was the one to deliver the whisky to Sosa's room."

Rachel sighed, not convinced of anything, but she knew arguing with Waverley when he was in triumphant mode would get her nowhere. She got up and left Waverley's office, angry and confused.

*You can be so patronising and obstinate sometimes, Chief Waverley*, she grumbled to herself as she took the stairs up to the main atrium and back to her room.

# Chapter 23

After dinner, Rachel went to meet Sarah and Jason in the Jazz Bar. They were already there by the time she arrived and a glass of martini and lemonade was on the table, waiting. They were talking quietly away from other guests, but the music was loud enough to drown out any other noise anyway. At any other time, Rachel would have felt awkward at intruding, but she assumed Jason was telling Sarah about the arrest.

"Did my parents go to bed?"

"Yes, they sent their apologies, but gave me strict instructions that we are to meet them for breakfast tomorrow before going ashore – you too, Jason."

"You mean Mum gave strict instructions!"

"I don't remember."

"Not convinced, but anyway I hear congratulations are in order. Well done, Rachel. You've done it again, although I have to say I'm surprised about it being Danielle. She always seemed pleasant, but I didn't know her that well. Bernard will be gutted when I tell him. He's quite fond of her, especially after hearing her story."

Sarah was bubbling over with excitement and words

were falling out of her mouth. Rachel flopped down in the chair and lifted the martini glass they had ordered for her.

"How is she?" Her question was aimed at Jason.

"Not good, and still protesting her innocence. The boss is happy, though, now his wife's in the clear."

"Good that someone's happy, then."

"Rachel, what's the matter? You should be pleased you've solved the case."

"I feel sorry for her, that's all. What will her family do now?"

"Are you sure that's all it is? I feel for her too, but she can't go around murdering people, no matter what they've done." Sarah took her hand. "Come on, cheer up. Carlos will be here soon and it's nearly Christmas."

"Okay, not that my beloved fiancé has contacted me yet." Rachel smiled and sipped her martini. Sarah was right, and everything did point towards Danielle. "But why do I feel like I'm missing something?"

"You're not missing anything and you're not going to put a dampener on our outing tomorrow, or on Christmas for that matter, so snap out of it, Rachel Prince."

Rachel laughed. "I'll consider myself told off. Watch out, Jason, when she gets like this, you just have to do as you're told."

"I'm beginning to see that. Sarah's right, though, Rachel. We followed the evidence and it all points to her.

She killed Stefan Sosa by spiking his whisky – maybe not totally for money, but perhaps that was what finally made her do it. Pash found out about the will, and then he tried to extort money from her daughter. She'd already killed one man that got in her way, it makes sense that she'd not let Pash take over from where Sosa left off. Whatever way you look at it, it was her."

"I keep trying to tell myself the same thing, but something doesn't sit right. You saw her, Jason, she was totally shocked when she heard Pash was dead."

"I give you that she came across as shocked, but she'd had since last night to practise what to say and how to react. The point is, someone was going to tell her today that Pash was dead. She'd have given it a lot of thought and prepared an appropriate response. I'm sure you've come across people like that in your line of work."

"I have. What you say does make sense. I'm just left with a few questions. I met her ashore today and she was crying."

"Guilt," postulated Jason.

"Possibly. She almost told me what had upset her, but ran away before I could find out."

"Have you considered that she might have been playing you? She's seen you with me and knows I'm dating Sarah. I think it was just an act. Forget it." Jason took a drink of tonic water.

"Please, Rachel," pleaded Sarah.

"Okay, you two, I'll try not to think about it. I liked

her, perhaps that's what I'm finding difficult. It's not often I like people who kill. I'm also struggling with the fact that she was justified – those men were evil, the way they preyed on the weak."

Sarah visibly relaxed and so did Rachel.

After drinks, Rachel excused herself. "I'll leave you two lovebirds to it and go and see if I can get hold of that man of mine. Meet you for breakfast, 8am sharp."

The happy couple laughed and Jason saluted. Rachel hesitated and she saw the flicker of a frown cross Sarah's fact.

"It's not about Danielle. I just wondered if you have noticed anything about your mum's eating. I don't ever remember her being so slow."

Sarah's cheeks reddened. "Now you mention it, she's not been herself, leaving food on her plate – something she never does at home, hates waste. I hope she's not ill – some nurse I am, I hadn't even noticed."

"It's probably the food on board. You know how rich it is," said Jason.

"Oh dear. I do hope so."

"Sorry," Rachel mouthed to Jason before leaving. Today was one of those days when her observation skills should be kept under wraps; she was not happy with the trail of damage they were leaving behind.

Rachel opted to take a stroll around the open decks upstairs, knowing sleep would escape her tonight. The hip felt much better, and if the killer really was locked up, she was not in any danger. Perhaps it was time to leave the first case behind after all. The niggling doubt festering in the back of her mind would have to quieten down sooner or later.

There was the question of how Pash had found out about the will, unless he had ransacked Sosa's room before she and Sarah had. But surely he would have removed evidence about his own blackmail if that was the case. The list of people who knew about the will was small, so it troubled her, but if Danielle was lying then it made sense that Sosa would have told her, and he too would have been likely to decide she should share the bounty with him. If that was the case, Danielle was definitely the killer.

"Admit it, Prince," she told herself. "You like her and don't want her to be guilty, but she is." A sense of relief followed and she pulled the phone out of her handbag and dialled.

"You must have read my mind." Carlos's cheery voice broke down all clouds that threatened to smother her.

"Carlos, I've missed you. I thought you might have called today."

"I'm sorry, darling. I left my phone behind in my cousin's hotel and had to go back for it. I'm on my way to Rome and will fly to Lanzarote tomorrow and stay in a hotel. I'll be with you on Christmas Eve."

"That's the best news I've had all week. Why can't you get to Gran Canaria?"

"All flights are fully booked. I only managed to get a seat on this one after charming a desk steward at the airport into giving me the first cancellation available for either place. I didn't want to risk losing this seat and one not turning up. I did look into getting from Lanzarote to Gran Canaria tomorrow, but decided to be patient. There's something magical about meeting up on Christmas Eve, don't you think?"

"Carlos, you watch too many American films, but yes, I'll take any time with you. Have you told Jason?"

"No, I was going to call him in the morning. Would you let him know?"

"Yes, of course. How come you finished the case so soon?"

"It was easy once I delved into the employment records and discovered a person whose ID didn't match official records. I managed to set up surveillance that none of the staff knew about and followed him. I just had to wait for his next move. I was getting impatient because I have been desperate to join you, but I caught him last night. He has given the police names of two people he was working with. It seems they were targeting three hotels, each of them working under false identities. My cousin is ecstatic, wanted me to stay for Christmas, but when I explained I could join the love of my life, she was happy to let me go."

"It's so good to hear your voice."

"Are you alright? You sound distracted."

"I'm tired. We can catch up on each other's news on Christmas Eve. I can't wait – do be careful travelling."

"Always, darling. I love you. Ciao."

"I love you too." She pressed the call end button feeling much happier.

After walking around the upper decks for another thirty minutes, listening to the sounds of the waves lapping against the side of the ship, Rachel decided to head down to her room. A couple passed by and said good evening. She heard the voices, but didn't see the faces as they hurried in the opposite direction. As she climbed into bed shortly afterwards, her head felt fuzzy – that voice. Why did she recognise it and why was it significant?

# Chapter 24

The number of staff serving in the Club Restaurant was diminishing and constantly changing. Mary told Rachel she had commented on the fact when a different wine waiter had served them wine over dinner the previous evening. On asking where Danielle Barcellos was, Mary said she had been fobbed off with the usual 'under the weather' excuse.

This morning, Mary asked Sacha if Danielle was still ill and he nodded.

"I told you, Gilbert. There's something going round this ship. I do hope you don't catch anything – it's bound to go on your chest, it always does."

"I feel perfectly healthy, my dear. Please don't worry yourself – it's winter, these things happen. Perhaps Pash and Danielle are among those who didn't have a flu vaccine."

"That's not likely. I don't think Bernard would allow it, Sarah says he's meticulous about following up on those who don't come for their vaccinations."

"I did hear him say he was chasing Danielle about being late for a vaccine," said Rachel.

"You see? There's nothing to be worrying about. Mary worries when she's not worried, don't you?"

"I suppose I do. Oh, I'm so looking forward to being on land again. I need firm ground under my feet. I do hope I won't be ill on the way home."

"Darling, let's enjoy the rest of our holiday first. Mary's worried about the three sea days that follow Lanzarote," Gilbert explained. "There's plenty of fresh air on the open decks, but she won't go out there."

"I worry about going overboard. I saw a film once where a storm came and people were swept out to sea."

Rachel marvelled at how fearful Mary had become. It wasn't something she'd had her down for. With that and the slow eating, Rachel sincerely hoped there was nothing wrong with Sarah's mum.

"I can see what you're thinking, Rachel Prince. I'm quite alright, but I might as well tell you before Sarah joins us. It's that time of life, my doctor says, the dreaded menopause. He wants to start me on HRT, but I didn't want to begin anything new until the cruise was over. I've been suffering anxiety attacks, hot sweats and I feel so dreadfully tired all the time. Please don't tell Sarah, she'll only worry. I've had blood tests and everything is fine, apart from my age."

"I see. I think you should tell Sarah how you feel, though. It will help her understand why you've been a bit—"

"A bit what?"

"Erm – off colour."

"Quite," said Gilbert, coming to Rachel's rescue. "Our daughter is astute, she will have noticed. We should tell her."

"I'll tell her when I'm ready, Gilbert. You just don't get it! It's not like it's an illness, is it?"

"But it feels like one to you and the doctor did explain that some women suffer more than others. I wanted her to start the HRT straight away," he said, turning to Rachel, "but she worries about trying anything new."

"Yes, and what would have happened if I'd suffered side effects in the middle of the ocean?"

Rachel laughed. "For someone whose daughter works with one of the most brilliant medical teams on the planet, you're not inspiring confidence."

"Well I think I've had quite enough of this conversation, but I will tell Sarah that I'm going through a natural transition due to my age. Thank you for reminding me, you two!"

Suitably rebuked, Rachel and Gilbert finished their coffee just as Sarah arrived.

"Where have you been? Where's Jason?" Mary asked.

"Sorry, Mum, I overslept. Jason will be with us anytime. Have you ordered?"

"Only just," Gilbert assured her.

Jason arrived and had a quick word with Sacha and the new maître d, who Rachel didn't recognise, before joining them.

"Sorry I'm late, I went to the gym."

Mishka arrived with a fresh pot of coffee for Jason and Sarah and took their orders. Jason asked for a full English breakfast.

"Bang goes my gym workout," he said as he smiled amicably.

"Did you manage to get hold of Carlos last night?" Sarah asked Rachel.

"Yes, he's joining us tomorrow. Is that alright, Jason? We're so grateful to you for putting him up."

"No problem. I'll contact head office before we go ashore and ask them to arrange for his ticket to be waiting at the terminal." Jason tucked into his breakfast, looking like he hadn't a care in the world. The Bradshaws would never suspect how hard he had been working over the past seven days. Sarah seemed relaxed now that someone was under arrest; it was only Rachel who remained ill at ease.

The nagging doubts hadn't gone away and this troubled her. Not wanting to upset the happy foursome, she resolved to keep the thoughts suppressed for the time being, but her investigation was nowhere near finished yet. Something about that couple from the previous night was significant, but for now, the reason for this eluded her.

"Rachel!" Sarah sounded cross. "You're at it again."

Rachel lifted her head to see Sarah frowning. Mary smiled. "Don't worry. Only one more day to wait and he'll be with you."

Rachel forced a smile, but Jason still cast a concerned glance her way every so often as they finished their breakfasts. It seemed he wasn't convinced it was Carlos on her mind, but the others were happy.

After breakfast, Jason left them to collect last-minute items from their rooms while he went to confirm Carlos Jacobi would be joining the ship as his guest the next day. Rachel picked up her notes briefly and went through them one last time before she headed down to the main atrium to meet the rest of the party.

They had decided to take the hop-on hop-off bus tour, giving them the option to either stay on or get off at their leisure. Both Jason and Sarah had been to Las Palmas before and were happy to direct the group.

"We have been so lucky with the weather," said Gilbert as they arrived on the dockside and made their way through port customs to the bus stop. He was right: yet another beautiful sunny day and clear blue sky greeted them this morning. Mary seemed happier, having told Rachel about her anxiety attacks, and hopefully she would tell Sarah soon. Sarah would feel bad that she had been impatient with her mother, but in the end it would bring them closer together again. They generally had a good relationship and talked about most things.

A bus was already at the stop and they managed to find seats on the open-air upper deck. Rachel studied the tour map. The round trip would take one and a half hours altogether, but they would want to get off and take in some sights.

They had managed to sit together on the back seat, and Mary and Gilbert had already worked out how to plug in and tune the earphones they had been provided with as they boarded. These would allow them to listen to commentary while they travelled. Commentary was provided in multiple languages, just like the tour buses that took visitors around London.

Once the bus left the stop and Sarah's parents were listening to the information through the radio, Rachel leaned over Sarah and caught Jason's attention.

"I've been meaning to tell you both about a telephone conversation I had with Marjorie the day after boarding."

"Oh Rachel, I remember you mentioning that Marjorie had tried to phone, but with everything else going on, it completely slipped my mind. Sorry."

Jason moved to the empty seat in front of Rachel and turned to listen attentively. After checking that the other bus passengers were busy with headphones or too far away to eavesdrop, Rachel filled them in on the concerns Marjorie had over her friends, Aaron and Felicity McCauley, and their son, Harry.

"It sounds serious enough," Jason said. "Why didn't you mention it before?"

Rachel felt her cheeks redden. "I kept meaning to, but every time I remembered it, something else was going on, and then it would slip my mind again. I think I also convinced myself that if Marjorie's friends are really in any danger, the daughter-in-law would at least wait for the return journey, or for a big party like the one taking place on Christmas Eve."

"What's the name of the son again?" Sarah asked.

"Harry McCauley," Rachel answered, lowering her voice.

"The name sounds familiar. I know – yes – he's been into surgery a couple of times complaining of indigestion and stomach pains."

"Would that fit with gradual poisoning?" asked Jason.

"Yes it would," she answered nervously. "With the benefit of hindsight, it would."

"Right, as soon as we get back to the ship, I suggest you tell Dr Bentley and I'll tell the boss. See what the doctor suggests you do about Harry. We'll find out what rooms they are all staying in, and I expect the boss will want to put Louise McCauley under surveillance. I'll try to set up a chance meeting for you to introduce yourself and warn the McCauleys, Rachel, unless the chief wants to do it a different way. At least if they're alert, we should be able to prevent any further murders from taking place on this particular cruise."

"Did I hear you say murder?" Mary Bradshaw had removed her headphones and caught the last few words.

"Jason was saying that if any more waiting staff go off sick, there's going to be a murder on this cruise," Rachel improvised.

"Oh well, you shouldn't joke about such things, you just never know. I don't like to tempt providence. Anyway, we're coming up to Vegueta – you said that would be a good place to get off, Sarah."

Sarah mock wiped her brow as her mother turned to wrestle her father's headphones from his ears and suggest he get ready to leave the bus. For the next few hours they walked around the old part of the capital and visited the cathedral, the town hall, the museum, then ambled towards the main square.

Rachel enjoyed the walking, despite some residual pain to her hip and ribs. During the walk, she snatched a few moments with Jason to discuss the case of the McCauleys in more detail. Relief washed through her at having got Marjorie's worry out in the open. She hadn't realised how much it had been weighing on her mind.

Jason was a mountain of strength and took his responsibility seriously. Rachel was so pleased her friend had found this man and hoped they would stay together.

"Are you sure you don't mind putting Carlos up for the rest of the trip?"

"No, it will be fun. I like him. I guess I'll need to fill him in on the murder case, though. He's bound to ask what I've been working on."

"Yes, I've been thinking about that too. I'll tell him first, if that's okay? I don't want him to think I'm hiding things from him; it doesn't help with trust."

Rachel immediately regretted her choice of words.

Jason's brow furrowed.

"I'm pleased. I wouldn't want to hide stuff from him. I'd hate it if Sarah hid anything from me."

"A thing she'd never do – unless it was a surprise, of course. It's a two-way street, though, Jason."

He paused a moment. "I know, I'm working on it."

"Working on what?" Sarah called from in front.

"Never you mind," said Rachel. "I'm sure you'll find out soon enough."

Jason took Sarah's hand as they arrived in the main square where they decided to find a place to eat. They passed a number of bars and cafés while walking and ended up eating in a tapas bar. Rachel opted for a vegetarian tapas, while Mary and Gilbert chose seafood. Jason suggested Gilbert try the local beer, although he himself ordered apple juice. Jason and Sarah chose to eat calamari, also local, as Sarah was fond of squid. Rachel joined Jason in a glass of apple juice while the two Bradshaw women chose tea. Afterwards they treated themselves to chocolate churros, which Rachel exclaimed were the best thing she had ever eaten.

They arrived back on board the *Coral Queen* at 4pm and Rachel couldn't help thinking excitedly as she walked up the gangway steps that tomorrow she would be joined by Carlos. For now, she and Jason had work to do to come up with a strategy that would protect the McCauley family while trapping Louise McCauley into giving herself away. Rachel was well aware how terribly wrong such plans could go if not managed properly.

# Chapter 25

Waverley knocked at the door of a luxury suite that Rachel was already familiar with. This was the suite she had occupied in the past when travelling with Marjorie. Marjorie usually took the mirror image one on the port side.

A well-built man in his late seventies opened the door wide, inviting them in. Waverley glanced across the rear corridor to make sure they hadn't been seen before ushering Rachel ahead. The familiar suite made Rachel feel at home immediately and she walked through to the living room where a petite woman stood, attempting poise but looking nervous. She assumed this must be Felicity McCauley.

"I am sorry to disturb you, Mr and Mrs McCauley, but as I explained on the telephone, it is important. May I introduce you to Rachel Prince? Rachel is a friend of Lady Marjorie Snellthorpe, whom I believe you know."

The couple visibly relaxed at the mention of Marjorie.

"Please take a seat, Chief Waverley, and you, Miss Prince. Can we offer you a drink?" Felicity spoke first.

"No thank you." Waverley took a seat and Rachel

followed his lead. The couple joined them.

"Perhaps you had better tell us what this is all about, chief," said Aaron McCauley. "Although, I think we can surmise it has something to do with the business we discussed with Marjorie last month."

"I'll let Rachel go first as she has the details."

Rachel thought it best to get straight to the point. "I received a call from Marjorie the day after we left Southampton. She was concerned for your welfare since discovering some unpleasant facts about your daughter-in-law from the private investigator you hired to look into matters for you. It appears he was wary of trying to contact you while you were on board the ship for fear of alerting your daughter-in-law."

"What unpleasant facts? Why are we only just hearing about this?"

"She believes your suspicions about Louise McCauley are well founded. The investigator has uncovered that she is indeed involved in an ongoing relationship with a man she has known for three years. The investigator also found evidence of research in Louise's office; research into poisons and accidents leading to death at sea." Rachel opted not to answer the second question, realising any excuse other than the truth would seem inappropriate.

Aaron took his wife's hand supportively. Felicity McCauley had turned pale.

"Do go on."

Rachel continued, "We don't have any further details, but both Marjorie and the PI believe your lives may be in danger."

"I see. So the woman plans to kill us before she kills our son, does she?"

Rachel swallowed hard. "That's what we believe, sir, yes."

"So why hasn't she made her move? She's actually been quite pleasant throughout the cruise. We were beginning to think we'd misjudged her, although there is always a nagging doubt as to why she decided to join us on the voyage at the eleventh hour."

"The problem is," Waverley took over, "we can't prove anything with the limited evidence we have, but we obviously don't want to wait until it's too late, so Rachel and myself have come up with a plan. But we need you to go along with it."

"You want to use us as bait?"

"Yes and no," said Rachel. "Firstly, can I ask whether we should tell your son about the findings?"

"Absolutely not," said Felicity sharply. "He would never believe you. He's besotted with the woman and would be furious with us for hiring an investigator. This would alienate him and he'd tell her immediately."

"I did suspect that might be the case, but we need to get him out of harm's way because we don't know if or when the poison might cause irreparable damage."

"How do you propose to do that?" asked Aaron.

"Here's what we'd like to do," said Waverley. "As unpleasant as it might sound, with your permission, I would like you to secretly administer an old-fashioned emetic called ipecac – you may remember it – into your son's drink at dinner this evening. He will be sick enough to call a doctor and our chief medical officer, who has been fully briefed, will have him admitted to the infirmary, explaining to his wife that he will need intravenous fluids to rehydrate him."

"We used to keep ipecac in the house in case the children accidentally drank poison. I do remember it, but hasn't it been found to be useless? Also I think I read that it can do harm. Your plan sounds a bit too drastic," said Felicity, paling again.

"Far less drastic than being poisoned to death," said Waverley.

"Is this emetic safe?"

"Dr Bentley assures me it will do no lasting damage, just an unpleasant couple of hours, but he, erm—" Waverley coughed.

"Yes?" said Aaron.

"He isn't keen to use the drug." Waverley looked dejected.

"Then we have to find another way. If the doctor is concerned, we refuse."

Waverley sighed heavily. "I need to be frank with you. I believe that by getting your son to safety, we will also be putting your lives in danger as your daughter-in-law might take advantage of the opportunity to make a murder attempt."

"It all sounds far-fetched to me, like something you see in a crass movie, but we would be happy with an alternative plan if it helps Harry. I'm prepared to take the risk. What about you, Felicity?"

"I hope you're wrong, chief, but yes, I'm willing to take the chance."

"I have another idea how we can make sure Harry is taken out of the situation, but I'll need to discuss it with Dr Bentley first," Rachel said.

"If the doctor agrees to your plan, Miss Prince, we consent." Aaron spoke and his wife nodded agreement.

"Good. Have you planned to go ashore tomorrow?" asked Waverley.

"Yes, we are all booked on an outing."

"If the doctor goes along with Rachel's alternative plan, we will ensure that he tells Louise that Harry will need to remain in hospital for forty-eight hours. That will give her the opportunity to come up with a scheme, if we're right. The doctor will take blood from your son and have it analysed, so if he is being poisoned, we will know what the substance is and how we can treat him. As your daughter-in-law has researched people going overboard, we believe she will attempt to send you both over from your balcony. The balcony is rear-facing and provides the perfect crime scene."

Rachel nudged Waverley as she sensed Felicity

McCauley was being given more information than she needed to hear.

"Apologies, Mrs McCauley. You have nothing to be concerned about. We will be watching your daughter-in-law closely. I would like permission for something else, though."

Waverley explained what he would like to do and the McCauleys gave their consent.

"Well that's settled, then. It's a shame Harry will be in hospital on Christmas Eve, but if that's what you think is required, we will go along with your plan," Aaron stood and poured himself a shot from the mini bar, "on condition the doctor agrees to what Miss Prince has in mind and that it will not put our son in any danger."

Rachel nodded. "It won't, you have my word."

"Marjorie trusts you, so your word is good enough for me, young lady."

"I am so sorry to have to put you through this situation, Mr and Mrs McCauley," said Waverley. "I will speak to the cruise line and I feel certain we can make up for the inconvenience to your holiday."

Waverley got up to leave and Rachel followed.

"That won't be necessary," said Aaron firmly. "If you're right, we will be indebted to you for saving our lives. If you're wrong – especially you, Miss Prince – Marjorie will get a piece of my mind."

Twinkling sky-blue eyes convinced Rachel that Marjorie had the best of friends in this couple.

Bernard was taking the on call for the nurses, so after dinner, Rachel met Sarah and Jason in the Jazz Bar, along with the Bradshaws who appeared to be settling in for a late night. Rachel was fidgety, wanting to know what had happened since her meeting with the McCauleys. Eventually, Mary yawned and Sarah looked up.

"You look tired, Mum. It's been a long day, why don't you go to bed?"

"Yes, all this sunshine in the winter is making me feel like I'm on holiday at last. I did enjoy today."

"What are you doing tomorrow?" asked Jason.

"We're just going to go for a walk into town and then along the beach. I've always wanted to paddle on Christmas Eve, now I can," answered Mary. "Will you be joining us, Rachel?"

Sarah's eyes widened in horror. "Mum!"

"Oh yes, of course. I forgot Carlos will be joining you. I expect you'll want to go out somewhere together."

Rachel nodded appreciatively. "We'll have a lot to catch up on."

"Well you have a wonderful day. We'll see you at dinner tomorrow evening, then."

"Jason and I will join you afterwards for the crew's Christmas show, remember?"

Mary nodded and Gilbert helped her up. Rachel

watched as they walked away hand in hand.

"You were so fidgety, Rachel, I'm surprised Mum didn't catch on."

"She would have thought it was excitement over Carlos coming anyway, so don't worry. Don't keep me in suspense any longer. What happened?"

"We let poor Harry McCauley enjoy his dinner before putting out an alert for him to contact the medical centre. He contacted reception and Graham met with him as planned. He told him that the batch of medication we had been treating him with had been recalled, and then insisted he be admitted to the infirmary for forty-eight hours' observation. It was a brilliant plan, Rachel, I don't know how you came up with it, but it worked and no harm done, apart from a bit of a disgruntled Harry McCauley. Although it was a half-hearted annoyance – he seemed almost relieved at being able to get some rest. You also saved Waverley and Graham from ending up at loggerheads."

"Not quite me. I was pleased when the McCauleys refused to go along with the chief's crackpot plan, so it's all worked out. How did Louise take it?"

"Put on a convincing act of the caring wife, so much so she almost fooled me. No wonder Harry is so taken in, she is an amazing actor. If I didn't know what Marjorie had told you, I'd think she was like any other doting wife. Graham encouraged her to stay after Mr and Mrs McCauley Snr returned to their room, just to be certain she wouldn't try anything tonight."

"The boss has pulled our undercover waitress from the Club Restaurant and put her on Louise's tail. She won't be able to go anywhere without being seen. He has also got someone watching the video footage coming from the parents' room. We installed it while they were at dinner. The equipment's now fully operational."

"So now all we have to do is wait until she makes an attempt on the poor couple's lives."

"That's about the sum of it," said Jason, putting his arm around Sarah. She hated this kind of thing.

"Don't worry, Sarah, she won't try anything until tomorrow night."

"You can't be certain of that, Rachel."

"Tonight, the McCauleys have gone to bed. Louise will need time to think about her original plan, whatever that was, versus this new opportunity. I think she'll use the time tomorrow to concoct a new plan, and when she does, we'll all be ready for her." The phone rang. "It's Carlos! See you tomorrow."

"Good luck with telling him what you've got yourself into," shouted Sarah.

Rachel put her tongue out at her friend and pressed the call answer button.

# Chapter 26

Rachel leapt out of bed at 6am, pulling on a pair of leggings and matching vest before heading up to the gym on deck sixteen. Her hip was feeling much better, and although she didn't want to risk running, she thought a workout would do her good. Jason would be meeting Carlos and checking him onboard at around 8am, which gave her time to exercise, shower and get ready to meet him for breakfast.

Following the workout, she felt calmer, although the fluttering of anticipation in her stomach would not be quietened. She opened the door to her stateroom and jumped in the shower. Once dressed, she decided to drink coffee on the balcony and watch the activity on the portside. She might even see Carlos boarding.

As she walked back inside, there was a knock at the door. Opening it, she expected to see Waverley, but she was swept up into the arms of the man she loved. He lifted her off the ground and walked inside.

"Carlos! I wasn't expecting you for another hour."

"I came early. Jason was good enough to get me registered earlier than planned. I dumped my bags, and he told me where to find you. I've missed you so much."

Rachel gazed into his sincere brown eyes and the love reflected there took her breath away. They kissed for what seemed like an eternity before he stopped and looked at her again.

"I think you should go away more often," she laughed.

"Jason tells me you have things to discuss with me, so before I get carried away, perhaps we should talk."

Rachel sensed the serious tone and poured him a coffee.

"Let's sit outside and I'll tell you all about it."

An hour later, Carlos was fully in the picture about all that had occurred during the cruise so far. The only thing she didn't mention was the attack and stabbing, feeling it would cause him unnecessary pain, and he would then object to her being involved in the flytrap set for Louise McCauley – if she were required.

After she finished, he sat back and whistled. "What is it about you and murder, Rachel? Don't you think you will be getting enough of this sort of thing when you're a DS without using every holiday for practice?"

"That's not fair! It's not like I go looking for trouble. You wouldn't want me to ignore injustice if I can do anything about it."

"I'm not sure, I would like you to live a long and healthy life, now and in the future."

"Carlos, what is it? You put yourself in danger all the time in your line of work, so you're not going to go all male protector on me, surely! You know that's not who I am."

"No, I don't want to do that, but I would like to think that if you're on holiday, I don't need to worry about you getting involved in murder every time. At least killer one is under arrest."

"Hmm." He had a point, but this conversation could head into a row if they weren't careful, so rather than spoil the moment they had experienced prior to it, she changed the subject. "How was your day in Lanzarote?"

"It was nice, but I thought we could explore together. How would you like a run along some volcanic sand?"

Pleased she hadn't mentioned the injuries, she answered, "I've not long been for a gym workout, but a long walk would be wonderful."

"A walk it is, then."

They headed up to the buffet to meet Jason and Sarah for breakfast as Rachel wanted to avoid the Club Restaurant. Bernard, Brigitte and Gwen were also present and delighted to meet Carlos again, having only met him briefly during her first cruise when she had got to know him under similar stressful circumstances. Jason shook his hand and winked, but Carlos shook his head. Rachel sensed he was still unhappy with her disclosure, but he would have to get over it. He should know by now that she would never shirk her responsibility, no matter how dangerous, and if he couldn't live with that – it didn't bear thinking about.

Sarah sensed the tension, but said nothing. Rachel was thankful as her friend would be more likely to agree with Carlos on this particular subject.

As it turned out, they had a pleasant breakfast before Carlos took her hand and suggested they go ashore. Once they were off ship, he relaxed again and became more carefree. If he noticed the slight slowness to her gait, he didn't mention it.

They walked hand in hand along the beach and felt the heat of the sun beating down on their exposed arms and legs, having both changed into shorts before leaving. After walking without saying much for three quarters of an hour, Carlos stopped.

"I'm sorry. I shouldn't have been angry earlier – it was just a surprise, that's all. I never want to change who you are, Rachel, and I know it's unfair for me to want to protect you when you must worry about me at the same time. I never saw myself as a chauvinist, but perhaps it's there, deep down in my male psyche."

"Carlos, I don't mind you wanting to protect me. I want to protect you too, but we must both do what we do and accept the risks, because if we don't our marriage will be over before it's started."

"I know that, Rachel." He took her hand and they walked again, but there was a quiet between them that had not been there before. On the one hand, she wanted to kick herself for getting involved in a murder investigation, but on the other, if Carlos was having doubts it was better to air them before they married. Her heart raced as fear of losing him threatened to overwhelm her. What had promised to be a beautiful day was turning into anything but, and as if the weather understood, a soft drizzle began to fall.

They stopped for lunch to take shelter and chatted about the case he had worked on and about his cousin, but the clouds forming in the sky were closing in on her heart. As they walked back to the ship, it was if they had become strangers, and as soon as they returned, she excused herself, needing to get away from him. He didn't try to stop her leaving and all the trust issues that she thought had gone returned with a vengeance.

Had he met someone else?

Entering her stateroom, she took another shower and changed into warmer clothes. It would be a few hours before they were due to meet the Bradshaws for dinner, time they clearly needed. This had never happened back home, so why the sudden change of heart? It wasn't making sense. Tears threatened to fall, but she fought them back, determined that whatever happened, she would not let her heart be broken again.

The telephone in her room broke through her sense of doom.

"Carlos—"

"Sorry, not Carlos. We're on, see you upstairs."

Rachel joined Jason outside Aaron and Felicity McCauley's suite and Jason ushered her into the couple's bedroom.

"They're expecting Louise any minute," he explained quietly.

"What happened?"

"Louise excused herself from the outing today, saying she felt down about Harry being in the infirmary, and our tail tells us she's been going around, chatting to passengers and telling anyone who would listen that she's on holiday with her husband and the in-laws. She's told them the in-laws are depressed about all sorts of things and are now overreacting to her husband being in the infirmary. On a few occasions, she told passengers she thought the couple had lost the will to live and was worried about their state of mind. Sarah tells me she's even been in the infirmary telling Harry his parents are depressed."

"Does Harry believe her?"

"I'm not sure; Sarah just says he's besotted, so he might do."

"Setting the scene for her to be absolved if they go overboard by implying they are suicidal. Very clever."

"Yep. An hour ago she called the McCauleys, saying that she wanted to speak with them and suggesting pre-dinner drinks."

Just as Jason finished speaking, they heard a knock at the door. Jason handed Rachel a set of earphones so she could listen in through the hidden microphone in the stateroom.

Initially there were the usual greetings.

"Did you have a good day out?" Louise asked.

"Yes, we're pleased you're feeling better," Aaron replied. "We've not long seen Harry – he seems alright, I hope the doctor lets him out soon."

"They said he'll be fine for Christmas dinner tomorrow. While he's away, I thought it might be a good time for me to tell you I'm sorry that we haven't always got on and I wondered if there was any chance we could make a new start of things?"

"That would be good. I think we were all a little shaken by how soon you came on the scene following Harry's divorce, but we can see how much you love each other. It's been obvious on this cruise." Felicity's voice was more shaky than her husband's. Louise didn't appear to notice.

"What say we drink to that? I've brought champagne – I'll pour."

Rachel and Jason couldn't see what was happening in the next room, but sensed that this would be when Louise would slip the couple a sedative. Waverley would be watching from the operations room and security officers were on standby. Rachel nodded grimly to Jason, who remained still.

"Are you alright, Felicity?" Aaron asked with slurred speech.

"I don't feel very well."

Rachel imagined Aaron was trying to get up as they

heard a chair move.

"What have you done?"

Louise laughed. "Time to go to sleep, you two – permanently. You should always trust your first instincts, you know?"

"You won't get away—" Aaron didn't appear to be able to finish his sentence.

Jason remained where he was, as did Rachel. The next thing they heard was another knock on the door, followed by a man's voice. Rachel's eyes widened; they hadn't expected an accomplice. She looked at Jason, wondering whether they should intervene. He was about to move when Louise's voice cut in.

"They'll be out for a good few hours. Give me forty minutes to wash and dress, then make a call from this room to the restaurant. Tell them you and your wife have decided to stay in this evening and to let Louise McCauley know. I'll be in the restaurant, waiting for the message. Then throw them over."

"Okay, you take the glasses back to your room."

"No," Louise hissed. "Throw them over now, no evidence."

Jason left the bedroom through the balcony door and waited for the man to open the doors in the lounge area. As soon as she heard this happen, Rachel opened the bedroom door and stopped Louise McCauley in her tracks. The woman's shocked expression changed from malice to concern in an instant.

"Please, you have to help. I found my mother- and father-in-law unconscious. They need help."

Rachel smiled as she heard the door behind her open, and Waverley, followed by Carlos, entered the room. Jason already had the male accomplice in an arm lock and Carlos cuffed him, smiling sheepishly at Rachel.

"What is this? These people need help."

"We're quite alright, really."

Louise almost passed out as Aaron and Felicity rose from where they had flopped back in their seats.

"But—"

"Ah yes," explained Waverley. "We have had you under surveillance all day, madam. The tablets were switched to harmless placebos while you were speaking so eloquently about your in-laws' state of mind around the ship today."

"I don't know what you're talking about."

"Perhaps the video footage we have will help you remember." Waverley played a small amount of footage on the laptop he carried and Louise McCauley put up no further resistance. "Thank you for bringing along an accomplice. Him we didn't know about, but we'll know so much more by the end of the evening."

"How did you know?" Louise asked the McCauleys.

"A private investigator and this young lady here. Thank you, Rachel – you saved our lives."

Rachel blushed while Louise glared at her.

"I think you will enjoy the rest of your cruise in our

brig. Separate rooms, I'm afraid." Waverley instructed Jason, "You can come with me." He then cuffed Louise and turned to the McCauleys. "The cameras will be removed while you have dinner. I'll join you afterwards to explain things to your son."

"Thank you, chief," said Aaron. "Thank you too, Miss Prince."

"Rachel, please. This is my fiancé Carlos who Marjorie told you about."

"Pleased to meet you, Carlos. You have quite the catch in this young lady."

Carlos gazed into Rachel's eyes. "Don't I know it! I hope you don't mind me intruding, Rachel, but I asked the chief if I could accompany him to make sure—"

"I was safe," Rachel finished for him, rolling her eyes at the McCauleys. "Time to leave, I think." She took Carlos's hand and they left the couple to digest the events they had just been through.

# Chapter 27

Carlos arrived at Rachel's stateroom, dressed in a smart grey evening suit with matching tie. He looked every bit the man she knew. The earlier events appeared to have blown away the wind and the rain between them, and the bad weather also left as the ship set sail for Southampton. After the late afternoon's excitement, they melded back into the engaged couple they had been, and Rachel was left wondering whether she'd imagined the tension earlier.

"You look beautiful, Rachel. May I escort you to dinner?"

Rachel had chosen her dress and look well, wanting to make the extra effort for the Christmas Eve party that would follow the evening show, and to remind Carlos what he would be missing if he chose to walk away. She knew she was being ridiculous entertaining such thoughts, but her compass remained very slightly off in terms of the security of their relationship. Tonight would hopefully get them back on track.

"You don't look so bad yourself. As my other date hasn't shown up, I guess I'll have to settle for you."

He grinned impishly. "Is that the man with the broken

kneecaps? I left him downstairs."

They joined the Bradshaws in the Club Restaurant and Mary Bradshaw couldn't disguise her delight at seeing Carlos on board, admonishing him continually for threatening to leave Rachel alone over Christmas. Rachel had already warned him not to say anything about the crimes she'd been investigating while the Bradshaws had been on board.

"I expect she's been bored senseless without me," he said casually.

"I wouldn't go that far," answered Mary. "But she hasn't quite been herself – miles away most of the time."

Carlos's eyes shone with mischief. Knowing full well what had been preoccupying Rachel, he was taking it in good spirit.

"I have been the same. It was hard to concentrate without her."

"Stop it, you two," said Rachel, kicking Carlos under the table. "How was your day in Lanzarote, Gilbert?"

"It was lovely. We got caught in a rain shower, but other than that it was pleasant. Mary wanted to stay ashore until the last minute, but I made sure we were at least close by. I didn't want to get left behind."

"It's only because I knew it was the final land day. Although, after all the trips we've taken over the last four days, I'm actually looking forward to three days at sea. We can explore the ship some more. I'm reliably informed that Christmas dinner is not to be missed. We even saw Santa in the main atrium on our way back on board. It was wonderful seeing children's excited faces while they queued for a chat and a present."

Rachel listened while Mary chatted excitedly with Carlos, who was encouraging the couple to tell him all about their experiences and outings. It was satisfying watching him enjoying a virtual cruise as they explained the ins and outs of every place they had been to. There was a hint of sadness in her heart that the first thing she'd told him about was murder and planned murder. Was that what she was becoming? Someone who no longer appreciated the beauty in the world? Perhaps that's what Carlos was afraid of.

The cruise had been enjoyable in many ways and she too had appreciated the few trips out, but she had been preoccupied. If she faced the truth, she enjoyed catching criminals more than she enjoyed anything else.

Carlos squeezed her hand, bringing her back to the present.

After dinner, Sarah and Jason arrived and they all headed to the theatre to watch the crew put on the show that Rachel had watched being rehearsed a couple of days before. They had been served by different waiters again throughout the evening, but Rachel assumed this was because Mishka and Sacha were involved in the play and had to attend a pre-show rehearsal.

Jason led the way to a row of reserved seats near the front. Sarah explained that she and Bernard, who hadn't yet arrived, might need to exit promptly should there be any emergencies. Gwen was also joining them while Alex covered the on call for the rest of the ship.

Bernard and Gwen turned up a few minutes later.

"I'm looking forward to resting my feet," announced the Australian senior nurse. "It's been one of those days."

Rachel sat between Sarah and Carlos, with Gwen next to the aisle and Jason on the other side of Sarah. The Bradshaws were next to Jason in more central seats. The excited chattering of passengers filled the air. Jason was drinking tonic water, Sarah and Bernard drank colas, and Gwen joined Rachel and the Bradshaws with the day's cocktail as she was off duty.

The lights were finally dimmed as the sound of music filled the two tiered theatre that spanned three decks at the front of the ship. It was time for the show to begin.

The crew put on a mesmerising performance and got a standing ovation. The whole show went off just as Dr Bentley had planned. He and the cruise director took a bow at the end, and passengers whooped and cheered as if they were at Carnegie Hall.

The whole cast was on stage when Rachel's head shot up. "Who's that woman talking to Sacha?" she asked Sarah.

"She's Frank's wife."

"Who's Frank?"

"He manages the casino, why?"

Rachel jumped up and slapped her head. She leaned

over Sarah and spoke to Jason.

"We need to get backstage. Call Waverley."

Jason spoke into his radio while cheers rang through the theatre. Rachel got up and Jason followed, leaving Carlos and Sarah looking bemused. Luckily, Mary and Gilbert were already chatting excitedly about the show with the people next to them and didn't notice Rachel's hasty departure.

Jason led the way to the rear of the theatre. "We need to speak to Sacha," Rachel explained.

By the time they arrived, Waverley was there, a little out of puff.

"What's going on?"

"Apparently we need to speak with Sacha Voronin."

Jason tracked the waiter down and told him to join them. As they made their way back to Waverley's office, Sacha's shoulders hunched. Waverley's confused expression showed as he asked the man to take a seat.

Before he got the opportunity to ask Rachel what was going on, Sacha spoke.

"How did you find out?"

Rachel answered, "When you and your sister – I thought she was your girlfriend at the time – passed me the other night, a memory nagged me. At first I imagined I recognised your voice – which I did in retrospect – but it was actually the shoes. You wear distinctive trainers with a fox painted on the toes. It was an image flashback that bothered me, not the voice. I saw the fox ever so briefly when I was tripped over on deck sixteen. When I saw you tonight, even from a distance, I remembered seeing the fox, and when I learned who the woman was on stage with you, I pieced it all together."

Waverley listened intently, staring at Rachel. "So this man is our killer, not Danielle Barcellos?"

"Correct. He killed both men to protect his sister." Rachel turned back to Sacha. "I assume the first killing was because Sosa was blackmailing your sister, and the second? You will perhaps enlighten us with the reason."

Sacha bowed his head. "Sosa was not satisfied with blackmailing Pash, he was also blackmailing my sister, Lola. I heard him bragging one day to Danielle about it. I waited for the right time. I knew Danielle would take him a new bottle of whisky while he was in London. I spiked the open bottle in his room, and when I saw her taking a fresh bottle from storage, I told Pash, knowing he would store the memory for his own use.Also it would help me get away with murder.

"Later that day, I searched Sosa's room and managed to get in the safe. He hadn't changed the code from original. I removed all photos and records of my sister and read through everything else in case I found something important. I also found a will that I didn't have time to read so I took it with me."

"You removed the epi-pens and returned them later, I presume?"

"Yes, just in case the medicine would help. I didn't

want him to get help."

"Why did you tell Pash about the will?"

"There was complication. My sister is pregnant, but doesn't know who is father. She told Pash that if the baby was mixed race, her husband would know about the affair and disown her. She wanted him to either pay for abortion or promise he would provide for her and the child if the child was Pash's and her husband divorced her. He refused, said she should have been more careful, and that now he had been promoted, he didn't want to put his job at risk. He told her if she told anyone the baby could be his, he would smear her name.

"I decided to tell Pash about the will as I knew he would demand some of the money from Danielle, and that he would remember the whisky bottle Danielle took to Sosa's room. It worked. Mishka and me saw Pash and Danielle have row."

"Afterwards you took her badge and planted it at the crime scene," said Rachel.

"That was lucky break for me, she left it in galley area of restaurant."

"Why did you choose to frame Danielle? She has a daughter."

"No-one liked her. We all knew she spied for Sosa – I did the others a favour by getting her away and saved myself at the same time."

"Except you didn't, did you? You're under arrest," snarled Waverley. "Goodridge, get this man out of my sight. Rachel, come with me please."

Waverley led Rachel to the room where Danielle was being held and opened the door. Rachel smiled at her.

"It's over – you're free."

Tears fell down Danielle's face as she hugged Rachel. "Thank you."

Rachel held her tight. "You're welcome. You can start again now."

Waverley coughed. "I apologise, Ms Barcellos. The real murderer is now in custody and Mishka will be sacked on return to Southampton, so you can begin again with a clean slate. I'll make sure you're moved to a different restaurant for now."

Danielle glared at the chief and walked away.

"I guess I deserved that."

"You did, but even I was almost convinced in the end. Sacha very nearly got away with it."

"But for Miss Rachel Prince, cruise ship sleuth," said Waverley, smiling.

# Chapter 28

The Christmas Eve party had been a resounding success, once Rachel and Jason had managed to convince the Bradshaws that they had both been taken short, and then struggled to find them again due to the crowds leaving the theatre. Carlos knew the full story, as did Sarah, and both were pleased that the real killer was now in the brig. Sarah was particularly pleased and wanted to tell Bernard straight away. Bernard had never believed the killer could be Danielle, so he was delighted. Rachel omitted the part about recognising the fox on the shoe from the day she was attacked. Feeling slightly guilty at holding out on Carlos, she decided that some things were best not known.

Now Christmas Day was here at last and the seas were relatively calm, considering the time of year, although whether that would continue when they reached the Bay of Biscay, no-one could know. Rachel spent most of the morning on the telephone, calling family while there was still a phone signal. Carlos had joined her for a room-service breakfast, and then left to call his own family and get ready for the big Christmas lunch.

Marjorie called just before noon.

"Felicity phoned me this morning to thank me for tipping you off, and she has asked me to thank you again on their behalf."

"Pleased to be of assistance," Rachel replied, good naturedly. "How did Harry take it? I haven't spoken to Waverley since yesterday."

"Badly, I'm afraid. It's hard to believe someone you love wants you dead. It will take time, but at least he isn't angry with his parents."

"That's good. They are a lovely couple."

"Speaking of parents, have you spoken to yours?"

"Not long got off the phone, as a matter of fact. The vicarage is feeding sixteen today."

"My goodness! How are you, dear? It must be difficult with Carlos away."

"He's not. He managed to wrap up his case and joined us yesterday. We're having Christmas dinner soon with Sarah, Jason and her family."

"Oh that is good news. I wondered who the two handsome young men Felicity mentioned were, I assumed one was Jason and knew the other couldn't be Chief Waverley. We're a few hours behind you and I'm about to go for breakfast. Jeremy sends his love. Happy Christmas, Rachel. See you when you get back."

"Happy Christmas, Marjorie."

After putting the phone down, she answered a knock at the door. Carlos was beaming from ear to ear.

"What is it?"

"You'll find out soon enough."

"I don't like surprises."

"Then it's a good thing I haven't arranged anything."

Rachel was bemused, but decided she wasn't going to get anything out of him, so she might as well let him have some fun.

They made their way down to the main atrium where pre-dinner cocktails and champagne were being served to every guest. Carlos led her to where the Bradshaws were already gathered, along with the medical team who were chatting to other guests. Waverley stood nearby.

Jason called the group to attention. "I would like to propose a toast."

Danielle gave Rachel and Sarah wide smiles and held out a tray of champagne. Before Jason had the opportunity to say anything, Sarah took a drink with her left hand and all jaws dropped open as the diamond shone brightly from her ring finger.

"To my fiancée, Sarah Bradshaw."

Rachel's heart burst with happiness and she gazed around at the joy before her. This was what Christmas was all about.

Rachel hugged Sarah. "Now that is the sort of surprise I like."

"I'm so happy, Rachel. I could burst. He asked my parents last night apparently and brought me a champagne breakfast this morning."

Rachel knew there would be plenty of time for the details, but for now she wanted to leave the happy couple to the congratulations of parents and friends.

Carlos took her hand and gently lifted his glass to hers, holding her gaze lovingly.

"Happy Christmas, darling."

They were going to be alright after all.

"Happy Christmas, Carlos!"

## THE END

# Author's Note

Thank you for reading *A Christmas Cruise Murder*, the fifth book in the *Rachel Prince Mystery* series. If you have enjoyed it, please leave an honest review on Amazon and/or any other platform you may use. I love receiving feedback from readers and can assure you that I read every review.

Keep an eye out for Book 6 in the *Rachel Prince Mystery* series. Working title: *Murderous Cruise Habit* is due for release in 2020.

Keep in touch:
Sign up for my no-spam newsletter at:
https://www.dawnbrookespublishing.com

Follow me on Facebook:
https://www.facebook.com/dawnbrookespublishing/

Follow me on Twitter:
@dawnbrookes1

Follow me on Pinterest:
https://www.pinterest.co.uk/dawnbrookespublishing

# Acknowledgements

Thank you to my editor Alison Jack, as always, for her kind comments about the book and for suggestions, corrections and amendments that make it a more polished read.

Thanks to my beta readers for comments and suggestions, and for their time given to reading the early drafts. I also offer thanks to those who read my books post edits as their comments are invaluable, picking up minor errors for correction.

Thanks to my immediate circle of friends, who are so patient with me when I'm absorbed in my fictional world, for your continued support in all my endeavours.

I have to say thank you to my cruise-loving friends for joining me on some of the most precious experiences of my life and to the cruise lines for making every holiday a special one.

# About the Author

Dawn Brookes is author of the *Rachel Prince Mystery* series, combining a unique blend of murder, cruising and medicine with a touch of romance.

Dawn has a 39-year nursing pedigree and takes regular cruise holidays, which she says are for research purposes! She brings these passions together with a Christian background and a love of clean crime to her writing.

The surname of her protagonist is in honour of her childhood dog, Prince, who used to put his head on her knee while she lost herself in books.

Bestselling author of *Hurry up Nurse: memoirs of nurse training in the 1970s* and *Hurry up Nurse 2: London calling*, Dawn worked as a hospital nurse, midwife, district nurse and community matron across her career. Before turning her hand to writing for a living, she had multiple articles published in professional journals and co-edited a nursing textbook.

She grew up in Leicester, later moved to London and Berkshire, but now lives in Derbyshire. Dawn holds a Bachelor's degree with Honours and a Master's degree in education. Writing across genres, she also writes for children. Dawn has a passion for nature and loves animals, especially dogs. Animals will continue to feature in her children's books as she believes caring for animals and nature helps children to become kinder human beings.

# Other Books by Dawn Brookes

## Rachel Prince Mysteries
A Cruise to Murder
Deadly Cruise
Killer Cruise
Dying to Cruise
A Christmas Cruise Murder

## Memoirs
Hurry up Nurse: memoirs of nurse training in the
1970s
Hurry up Nurse 2: London calling
Hurry up Nurse 3: More adventures in the life of a
student nurse

## Coming in 2020
Book 6 in the *Rachel Prince Mystery* series
Murderous Cruise Habit

Look out for New Crime Novel Series in 2020
Book 1 Murder in Chaddesden Wood

## Picture Books for Children

Ava & Oliver's Bonfire Night Adventure
Ava & Oliver's Christmas Nativity Adventure
Danny the Caterpillar
Gerry the One-Eared Cat

Made in the USA
Columbia, SC
26 March 2023